D0312324

MURDER
IS AN ART

Murder Is an Art

Bill Crider

THOMAS
DUNNE
BOOKS

ST. MARTIN'S PRESS
NEW YORK

THOMAS DUNNE BOOKS.
An imprint of St. Martin's Press.

MURDER IS AN ART. Copyright © 1999 by Bill Crider. All
rights reserved. Printed in the United States of America. No
part of this book may be used or reproduced in any manner
whatsoever without written permission except in the case of
brief quotations embodied in critical articles or reviews. For
information, address St. Martin's Press, 175 Fifth Avenue,
New York, N.Y. 10010.

Library of Congress Cataloging-in-Publication Data

Crider, Bill.
    Murder is an art / Bill Crider.
        p.   cm.
    "Thomas Dunne books"—T.p. verso.
    ISBN 0-312-19927-9
    I. Title.
PS3553.R497M86   1999
813'.54—dc21   98-41786
                                                          CIP

First Edition: April 1999

10   9   8   7   6   5   4   3   2

MURDER
IS AN ART

1

---◆---

When Perry "A. B. D." Johnson strode into the office of Sally Good, chair of the Division of Arts and Humanities at Hughes Community College, he was in a state of medium dudgeon.

His condition came as no surprise to Sally. With A. B. D. Johnson, as Roseanne Roseannadanna used to say, it was always something.

A. B. D. arrived on campus at 7:30 A.M. every day, already in a state of low dudgeon. He worked his way up as the day went along, usually reaching high dudgeon somewhere between 2:30 and 3 P.M., at which time he went home and took out his frustrations either by grading his students' papers or working on his doctoral dissertation.

His dissertation, or rather the fact of his dissertation's incompleteness, was the reason for his being known all over campus by the initials A. B. D. They stood for "All But Dissertation," a condition that described exactly how far Johnson had advanced in graduate school. He had finished all his course work and passed both his minor and major oral examinations seventeen years previously. He had then left graduate school and accepted a job at Hughes.

Ever since his arrival on campus, A. B. D. had supposedly been working toward the completion of his dissertation in his spare time. The topic was rumored to be phallic imagery in the "Calamus" poems of Walt Whitman, though no one was certain. No one had ever seen a copy of the work in progress, and A. B. D. resolutely refused to discuss his ideas with anyone, possibly for fear that his listener might steal them and publish them to worldwide scholarly acclaim.

A. B. D. had gone through two wives, four dissertation directors, two division chairs, and three deans since arriving at Hughes, but as far as anyone knew, he had made little progress on his magnum opus.

He had, however, achieved what Sally believed to be the world record for pleading with, cajoling, wheedling, and outright begging graduate-school administrators to allow him to continue in the program without having to repeat his course work.

He was, in Sally's opinion, perfectly equipped for begging and pleading—baggy clothes, big sad eyes, longish black hair (going slightly gray) that flopped over his forehead, and a hang-dog face that reminded Sally of either Richard Nixon or Walter Matthau. She was never quite sure.

At any rate, A. B. D. had always been successful in his petitioning. Deadline after deadline had come and gone, and he had failed to meet a single one. Yet he persevered in his work, or claimed to, and Sally supposed she had to give him credit for doing that much.

She looked up at his red, cheerless face and resisted the impulse to say what she really wanted to say, which was "What is it *this* time, A. B. D.?"

Instead, she smiled as if she were actually glad to see

him and said, "Good morning, Mr. Johnson. How are you today?"

He didn't bother to answer the question. He said, "Val Hurley has a new chair."

Val Hurley was the chair of the Art Department, and it was true that he had a new chair. Sally acknowledged the fact.

A. B. D. looked at her accusingly. "It's an executive chair. It's all leather. It has a pneumatic seat. It has ball bearings in the rollers."

Sally continued to smile, even though she was sure she knew where the conversation was heading. "That's right. It's a very nice chair."

A. B. D. Johnson's face got redder. It seemed almost certain that today he was going to reach high dudgeon way ahead of schedule.

"*I* don't have a new chair," he said. "I have the same old chair that I've been using for the last seventeen years, ever since I came to Hughes. The vinyl one that's practically held together with duct tape I bought myself. The one with the frozen rollers. The one that won't even lean back without tipping over."

For just a moment, Sally felt a little guilty and self-conscious, sitting there in her own executive chair, which was actually a little nicer than the one Val Hurley had bought. The feeling passed quickly, however.

"You could have had a new chair if you'd wanted one," she told Johnson. "When I was working on the departmental budget, I asked everyone to let me know what office equipment they needed. Val Hurley included a new chair in his departmental budget, and I would have been glad to include one for you in our budget if you'd asked."

"I'm sure you would have." A. B. D.'s voice began to rise, and his jowls shook just the tiniest bit. "I'm sure you would have, even though it's common knowledge that the faculty hasn't had a raise in two years and the enrollment is dropping and the whole school is going down the financial tubes. At least that's what Fieldstone keeps telling us."

There was a sarcastic edge to the last sentence that indicated that A. B. D. Johnson was not merely a simpleton to be taken in by anything that Harold Fieldstone, the college president, might say about the school's finances. A. B. D. was much too shrewd a fellow to believe a scum administrator.

"You're exaggerating," Sally said. "It's true that we haven't had a raise lately, and it's true that the enrollment is cause for concern, but that doesn't mean we can't have decent chairs for our faculty members."

"Hah!" A. B. D.'s jowls shook even more, and Sally made a sudden realization: it was Nixon whom A. B. D. most resembled.

"What it means," A. B. D. continued, "is that we can have whatever the president wants us to have around here. He likes things like fancy chairs and new cars. Did you know that Campus Security has two new cars?"

Sally knew. "They were bought with money brought in from the sale of parking permits."

"Hah!" The jowls waggled. "That money could have gone into raises for the faculty just as easily as it could have gone into new cars for the cops."

"We're getting away from the subject," Sally said.

She couldn't fool A. B. D. He said, "It's all the same subject, as you very well know, but never mind that. I just wanted you to understand that I'm going to speak to Val, and I'm going to write a memo to the president about this matter. Fieldstone thinks he can get away with this, but he can't."

"The president didn't have anything to do with getting Val a new chair," Sally said. "As Val's supervisor, I approved his departmental budget. Then I sent it to Dean Naylor, who also approved it. The president probably doesn't even know about the chair."

A. B. D. Johnson looked at her with pity. "That's what he'd *like* us to believe," he said. Then he turned and stalked away.

Sally sighed and leaned back in her own executive chair. It was going to be one of those days. There might even be a repetition of the parking incident memo, which had been written after A. B. D. saw a student parking in a space reserved for the faculty.

A. B. D. had been furious, especially because when he had called the student's attention to the transgression, the young man had said, "What's it to ya?"

A. B. D. had reached high dudgeon in record time that day, storming into Sally's office to demand that the student be shot or, failing that, withdrawn from all his classes.

"Shooting him would teach the students a wonderful lesson," A. B. D. insisted. "We should probably shoot one student at the beginning of each semester as an example to the others of what could happen if they don't toe the line. It would solve a world of problems around here."

Sally was pretty sure that A. B. D. was kidding, but he sounded awfully serious.

"I'm not sure the Board would approve," she said.

A. B. D. was ready for that one. "Let Fieldstone explain it to them. That's his job, isn't it?"

Sally had talked with A. B. D. a few minutes longer and persuaded him that the best thing to do, if he was still feeling vindictive, would be to report the student to Campus Security so someone could ticket the student's car.

A. B. D. had stalked away toward the Security Office, clearly disappointed in Sally's lack of initiative. Two days later, Sally had received a call from President Fieldstone.

"I have a memo here from one of your faculty members,"

Fieldstone said. "What do you know about it?"

It was an ominous question since Fieldstone didn't like to receive memos from faculty members, and it was doubly ominous since Sally had no idea what he was talking about. If there was anything Fieldstone liked less than receiving memos, it was a division chair who didn't know what was going on in her own division.

So instead of answering the question, Sally asked, "Which faculty member?"

"Perry Johnson," Fieldstone said. He never called him A. B. D.

Sally remembered the parking incident at once. "Complaining about the student car in the faculty parking spot?"

"Indeed. He seems quite upset. Do you think his idea has any merit?"

Sally didn't believe that even A. B. D. would be stupid enough to suggest shooting a student in a written memo. Still, she thought she'd better be cautious.

"What idea?" she asked.

"The idea of putting something called 'the boot' on cars that are parked illegally."

Sally had heard about the boot before. Big-city police sometimes used it to immobilize the cars of parking violators. She told Fieldstone that she didn't think it was something that was needed on a college campus.

"My thought exactly. We don't want to antagonize our students; they're our bread and butter." Fieldstone paused and then said, "Is there anything . . . wrong with Johnson? You aren't pressuring him to finish his dissertation, are you?"

A year or so earlier, Johnson had written a memo to complain that he felt under tremendous pressure from "certain administrators and department chairs" to complete his dissertation so as to "make the faculty look better" when accreditation agencies visited the school. Sally had never figured out who had been pressuring Johnson, and no one had ever admitted it.

"I haven't been pressuring anyone," she said. "Mr. Johnson's just excitable."

"Try to calm him down, then. I don't like having to reply to memos like this one."

Sally started to tell Fieldstone that he didn't have to reply, but she thought better of it. It wouldn't do any good. Fieldstone never let anything go without a reply. So she assured him that A. B. D. wouldn't be writing any more memos for a while.

And now Val Hurley's new chair was going to make a liar out of her. Maybe A. B. D.'s idea about having a student shot could be revised somewhat, Sally thought. Instead of shooting a student, the division chairs could draw straws, with the winner getting to shoot one faculty member.

No, it would never work. Fieldstone could never get it past the Board. Unless, of course, he reminded them of the payroll reductions involved . . .

Sally shook her head and smiled to herself. The Board would never go for it, but it was a pleasant fantasy. Now, however, she had to do something practical.

Like warn Val Hurley that A. B. D. was on the warpath.

2

Sally pushed aside the stack of papers that nearly covered her telephone and pulled the phone across the desk to her. She could never remember whether she was right-brained or left-brained, but whichever it was, she simply couldn't manage to keep her desk uncluttered for more than twenty minutes.

Things just seemed to pile up, and her desk was always nearly hidden beneath piles of student papers and exams, syllabuses, schedule forms, books, purchase orders, magazines, memos, letters, empty envelopes, class notes, the odd Hershey wrapper, and God knows what else. Her old college transcripts might be in there somewhere for all she knew, though she certainly hoped not. She wouldn't want anyone to find out about that D she'd made in algebra when she was a freshman.

She punched in Val Hurley's number and let the phone ring five times before hanging up. She couldn't remember Val's schedule, and God knows where her copy of it was, but she didn't believe he had a class at eleven o'clock on Tuesdays.

He could be anywhere, however—in the restroom, in the art lab, in the library, in the bookstore. There was no use trying to track him down. He'd just deal with it if A. B. D. got to him before Sally did.

Sally pushed the phone back across the desk through the accumulation of papers and looked around her office. She had been at Hughes Community College for six years, and she had brought all her books with her from her previous school. With those added to the ones she had acquired since arriving, the bookshelves were as bad as her desk. Worse, maybe.

There were books stacked on top of books and in front of books. There were books on the typing table and on top of the IBM Selectric that hadn't been used since Sally moved into the office. There were books on the filing cabinets and on the computer desk. There were even books in a grocery bag on the floor.

Sally was wondering what she was going to do if she ever got any more books, which of course she inevitably would, when the telephone rang.

She dragged the phone back through the papers, picked up the receiver, and said, "Sally Good."

"Please hold for Dr. Fieldstone," said the voice of Eva Dillon, Fieldstone's secretary.

A chill went through Sally as it always did when Fieldstone called, despite the fact that Eva had a very pleasant telephone voice, the kind that made you think she was probably a svelte brunette of dignified mien.

The dignified part was right, and Eva was definitely a brunette, but she wasn't svelte. She had a serious chocolate habit and kept a bag of king-size Snickers bars in the bottom drawer of her desk. She had once confessed to Sally that she ate at least three a day. Sally could identify with this, though she managed to keep her own chocolate consumption down to one Hershey bar with almonds a day. Well, most days, anyway.

While she was waiting for Dr. Fieldstone to come on the line and give her the bad news, whatever it was, Sally said "shit" under her breath a couple of times. She was afraid that instead of writing a memo, A. B. D. had gone straight to Fieldstone's office to complain about Val Hurley's new chair. That would be even worse than writing a memo. Although Fieldstone liked to talk about his "open-door policy" in every faculty meeting and go on at length about how faculty members were always welcome to drop in to see him, he didn't actually like for them to drop in on him at all. He especially didn't like for them to drop in if they had complaints.

"Dr. Good?" Fieldstone said.

That was a bad sign. When he was in a good mood, he used her first name.

"Yes?" she said.

"Could you please come over to my office for a moment?"

Uh-oh. A really bad sign. Otherwise, he would have had Eva ask her to come over. That damned A. B. D. Johnson.

"Of course," she said. "I'll be right there."

"Thank you."

Fieldstone hung up, and Sally leaned back in her chair, which didn't seem quite as comfortable as it had earlier. She sat for a few seconds and straightened some of the papers on her desk, a futile task if ever there was one. But she wasn't going to give Fieldstone the satisfaction of her rushing over.

After she had sorted some of her students' homework into separate stacks, she stood up, made sure her blouse was tucked in, and walked into the hallway, which was practically deserted, as it always was during classes. Most of the faculty members who weren't teaching at that hour were in their offices grading papers or surfing the Internet, and the students who didn't have class were either in the cafeteria drinking coffee or in the game room shooting pool.

Sally walked down the hall, the soles of her sensible shoes

squeaking a little on the tiles. The only person in sight was Jorge "Rooster" Rodriguez, the only convicted killer of Sally's acquaintance. He had just come out of his office, and when he saw Sally, he stopped to wait for her.

"You get a call from the Big Guy, too?" he asked.

Jorge had a high-pitched voice that didn't fit at all with his appearance, considering that he looked like a walking advertisement for steroid consumption. His upper body was huge and solid, tapering down to a waist so narrow that Sally had more than once regarded it with a twinge of envy.

She wasn't envious of the rest of him, however. He seemed about to burst out of the dark suit that concealed the elaborate tattoos on his arms. Sally had seen the tattoos in the summer when Jorge wore short sleeves. His arms were covered with snakes that coiled around his biceps; hearts pierced by daggers; weeping eyes; skulls; spiders.

There was supposedly another tattoo on his back, the tattoo that had given him his nickname. Sally hadn't seen that one. She'd heard about it from Troy Beauchamp, one of Sally's English instructors, who had seen Jorge working out in the gym.

"I swear to God," Troy had told her. "It just about covers his back. It's this huge rooster pecking on the eyes of a corpse. There's no color in it except for the red in the rooster's comb and the blood dripping from the corpse's eye sockets. Creepy? Amen. And Jorge's muscles? Jesus. You wouldn't believe the way he looks. He's like a Russian Olympic weight lifter."

Weights had a lot to do with Jorge's appearance, all right. He'd done a lot of lifting while serving out his sentence in one of the high-security units of the Texas Department of Criminal Justice. He'd also earned three degrees during his stay there: his associate's, his bachelor's, and his master's.

Jorge, in other words, had profited from the two primary things that the state legislators, and not a few of the state's citizens, from time to time wanted to deprive prisoners of: weight lifting and education. He still worked out at least an hour a day in the college gym, and he was working on his doctorate at the University of Houston.

"Fieldstone called, all right," Sally told him, "but he didn't say what he wanted."

"Of course not. That's part of his technique, a power thing. Keeps people off balance."

Sally silently agreed. Jorge had pretty good insights into people, a talent that had probably stood him in good stead while he was in the crossbar hotel.

"Did he say anything to you?" she asked.

"Just that he wanted to see me in his office. It must have something to do with the prisons, though, if I'm involved."

Sally nodded. Hughes Community College offered classes in several of the nearby prison units. The program had begun in a small way, but it had grown to the point that it required its own coordinator. That was where Jorge came in. Who better to deal with inmates, wardens, and prison educational personnel than a product of the system? The college's personnel officer had begun recruiting Jorge even before his release.

"Any lockdowns?" she asked. "Escapes? Problems in any of the classes?"

Jorge shook his head. He had thick black hair pulled back into a little ponytail. With the ponytail and the bulging suit, he looked a little like a B-movie drug dealer. The tassels on his shoes only added to the picture. If he'd been carrying a pistol in a shoulder holster, he would have been perfect.

"If it's not any of the usual stuff, what could it be?" Sally asked.

"I guess we'll just have to wait and let Fieldstone tell us that," Jorge said.

3

―――

Fieldstone's office was in the Administration Building, so Sally and Jorge had to go outside, not always a pleasant prospect when you live near the Texas Gulf Coast. In the summer, the weather was generally intolerably hot and muggy, and in the fall and spring, it was lukewarm and muggy. There wasn't much of a winter to speak of, but it was muggy, too.

However, now and then a cool front would push through, the sky would clear, the sun would shine, and the air would be pleasantly dry. It was that way as Sally and Jorge crossed the quadrangle to the Ad Building.

"It's a great day to be outside, isn't it?" Sally said.

Jorge said, "Any day is a great day to be outside."

Sally immediately felt guilty. She was just making conversation; she hadn't meant to remind Jorge of his prison experience. However long it had lasted, and the rumors about that varied, it couldn't have been pleasant.

But Jorge hadn't spent his time in solitary confinement or whatever they called it now—administrative segregation, maybe. Sally wasn't always up to date on prison terminology. At any rate, Jorge hadn't been inside a building all the time; surely he had been allowed an occasional walk outside in the yard.

She thought about asking him, but she didn't know how to go about it. Neither did anyone else, for while everyone was curious about Jorge's prison experience, they found him too intimidating to ask about such a personal thing.

He wasn't deliberately intimidating, but his size put people off. He wasn't just muscular; he was tall. Sally was five-seven, but her head barely reached the top of Jorge's shoulders.

And it wasn't as if he'd been in the slammer because he'd been caught driving ten miles over the speed limit on the Interstate; he had served time for murder. He might have seemed more approachable if he had been imprisoned for some drug-related offense, or possibly even something more serious—armed robbery, say. But murder was a little tricky to work into the conversation.

Like the stories about the length of time Jorge had spent behind bars, the stories about the exact nature of his crime varied. Oh, there was no doubt about the murder. That was well established. But no one seemed to know for sure just exactly what the circumstances had been.

One story had it that Jorge had killed his wife's lover. Troy Beauchamp favored that one, and Sally had heard him tell it more than once in the faculty lounge.

"The way I heard it is that he came home early from work one day," Troy had said. "And he caught his wife in bed with another man."

"What kind of work did he do?" asked Vera Vaughn.

Vera was a tall, stout blonde who taught sociology and dressed in leather a lot—leather skirts, leather pants, leather jackets. Sally's opinion was that if the college ever did a stage production of *Ilsa, She Wolf of the SS*, Vera would be a shoo-in for the title role.

Vera also had strong feminist leanings and occasionally expressed convictions that Sally thought were based more on emotion and speculation than on facts and research. For instance, Vera believed that the top women marathoners consistently finished behind the top men only because of social and cultural conditioning.

"Who cares what kind of work Jorge did?" Troy asked.

"It could be important," Vera answered. "A man's self-image is often related to his job. Jorge could have been driven to murder because of low self-esteem."

Troy grimaced. "I think he was a garage mechanic or something. He might have gotten his hands dirty, but he probably made more money in a week than I do in a month. Anyway, he came home early, and—"

"I don't think mechanics ever get off work early," Gary Borden said.

Gary taught psychology. He, or at least his wardrobe, had never emerged from the 1970s. He wore Buddy Holly glasses and dressed like a member of the cast of *The Bob Newhart Show*, the one where Bob played a psychologist. The lapels of his sports jackets stretched nearly to his armpits, and his ties were almost as wide. He liked to joke that he was related to Bob's neighbor Howard.

"When I take a car in to get it fixed," Gary went on, "I sometimes get a call to come by and pick it up at six-thirty or seven in the evening. Those guys put in long hours."

"Who cares what kind of job he had or what kind of hours he put in?" Troy asked. "The thing is that whatever he did, he got off early, he went home, and he caught his wife in the bedroom with this guy. Pulled him right off her and beat him to a bloody pulp with his bare hands."

Sally could almost picture it, Jorge standing there in greasy coveralls, his big hands like mallets, grease in the creases of his skin and under his fingernails. He was silently looking down at the battered body of the man who had been making illicit love to his wife. She wondered if he felt remorse.

"The wife called 911 while it was going on," Troy said. "But by the time the cops got there, it was too late."

"The cops always show up too late," Gary said.

Vera had a different slant on things. "I thought that in Texas, it was perfectly all right to kill your wife's lover if you caught them in the act. A typical example of how males manipulate the law, in my opinion."

"It's not all right," Gary said. "I mean, it's definitely against the law. But I've heard you usually get no-billed by the grand jury. Anyway, that's not the story I heard about Jorge."

"Then you heard wrong," Troy said.

Troy liked gossip, but he always liked to think that his version of events was the correct one, whether it was or not. He didn't like to be contradicted.

"Tell us what you heard," Sally said, always ready to get a new slant on things involving Jorge. She was intimidated by him, but she had to admit that he was interesting.

"I heard he killed some kid with a baseball bat," Gary said.

"An aluminum bat or a wooden one?" Troy asked, possibly in revenge.

Gary looked thoughtful, the way he might if some student in his class had raised his hand in the middle of a discussion of cognitive dissonance to ask when the winter break began.

"Gee, that's a very good question, Troy. I never thought about it before. It was probably wood, but it might have been aluminum. Either way, the results were the same."

"So tell us the story," Vera said. She didn't like interruptions unless she was the one doing the interrupting.

"It happened when he was just a kid," Gary said. "In San Antonio; some kind of gang-related thing. Some other kid had raped Jorge's sister—"

18

"Typical of a male gang member's aggression and hostility toward women," Vera said.

"Sure," Gary agreed. "Anyway, the cops couldn't pin it on him. He got some of the other gang members to swear he was playing cards with them when it happened, and it came down to her word against his and eight or ten other guys'. Jorge started in on the witnesses first, beating them up and making them promise they'd recant. When the rapist heard about it, he went after Jorge with a gun."

"Gun versus bat for the honor of a woman," Troy said. "Sounds like the plot of a bad black-and-white American-International movie from 1957."

"Were there any good American-International movies?" Vera asked.

"We could ask Jack Neville," Sally said.

Neville was as much a product of the fifties as Borden was of the sixties. He could spend hours arguing whether Fabian's musical efforts had held up better after forty years than Frankie Avalon's.

"I'd rather not," Gary said. "Do you want to hear about this or just forget it?"

"I'm sorry," Sally said. "I want to hear about it."

Gary looked at Troy, who nodded. Vera just smiled, cruelly, which was the only way she *could* smile.

"All right, then," Gary said. "The way I heard it, the other kid shot Jorge twice, but Jorge still managed to get to him with the bat. Smashed his head like a pumpkin."

"Smashing Pumpkins," Troy said. "Sounds like a good name for a singing group."

Gary looked at him blankly.

"Never mind," Troy said. "I forgot that you were a Moby Grape fan."

"Tell us more about smashing the head," Vera said.

There was a look in Vera's eyes that made Sally feel vaguely queasy, though not as queasy as the image of Jorge bleeding from his not-quite-mortal bullet wounds as he stood looking down at the crushed head leaking blood and fluid out onto the dark concrete of some back alley in San Antonio. She wondered if Troy had seen the bullet scars in the gym, but this probably wasn't the time to ask.

"That's the whole story," Gary said. "More or less, anyway. Somebody took Jorge to the emergency room, and the cops arrested him."

"Couldn't be true," Troy said. "The way you tell it, it was a clear-cut case of self-defense. Jorge would never have been sent away for murder if it had happened that way. It happened the way *I* said. Trust me."

As colorful as both stories were and as convincing as they sounded, Sally wasn't sure that either of them was even vaguely connected to reality. She'd heard other stories, too, and most of them were just as sensational as the two Troy and Gary had told. But nothing she'd heard had the ring of absolute truth. Someday, maybe she'd find out what had really happened.

But not right now. Right now she had to deal with Fieldstone.

4

Eva Dillon was behind her desk when Jorge and Sally entered the Ad Building. Sally thought she detected a telltale trace of chocolate at the corner of Eva's mouth, but she didn't mention it.

She said, "Dr. Fieldstone wanted to see us."

Eva nodded. "Go right in."

Sally opened the door and preceded Jorge into the president's office. The dark wood walls were covered with plaques presented to Fieldstone by various civic groups, interspersed with enlarged photographs of Texas wildflowers taken by Fieldstone himself. An avid amateur photographer, he took weekend trips every spring to get his glossy shots of bluebonnets, Indian paintbrushes, and Indian blankets.

Fieldstone sat behind a desk that wasn't quite as large as the deck of an aircraft carrier, in a chair that made Sally's executive model look as if it had been put together by the only English major in a high school crafts class. Fieldstone was wearing a dark suit that must have cost at least nine hundred dollars, along with a starched white shirt and an Endangered Species tie.

On the couch to his left sat Val Hurley and James Naylor, the academic dean, while on the couch in front of the desk was a man Sally recognized, though she had never met him.

His name was Roy Don Talon, and he was a local automobile dealer who'd made a fortune thanks to a series of TV ads in which he told potential customers in Houston to "Drive to *Hughes* for *huge* savings."

Sally would have liked to blame Talon for the fact that something like sixty percent of her students spelled the name of the school "Huge Community College," but it probably wasn't entirely his fault.

The fact that he dressed like a performer on the Grand Ol' Opry in the 1950s *was* his fault, however. He wore a sequined Western-cut jacket, matching pants, and cowboy boots—the same outfit he wore for his commercials. His ten-gallon hat was beside him on the couch. Maybe he was keeping up his image, but Sally thought it was a little much.

All four of the men stood when Sally walked into the room, a gesture that she knew was meant in the best possible way, so she didn't take offense. Vera Vaughn would probably have cut them off at the knees.

"Dr. Sally Good, chair of Arts and Humanities, and Mr. Jorge Rodriguez, who's in charge of our prison program," Dr. Fieldstone announced. "You two know Dr. Naylor and Mr. Hurley. This is Roy Don Talon."

"Howdy, ma'am," Talon said, sticking out his hand to Sally, who shook it quickly and let it go. It was cool and dry, and she felt as if she were shaking hands with a lizard.

Jorge didn't let go of Talon's hand quite so soon, and Sally noticed a narrowing of Talon's eyes. She wondered if Jorge was showing off his grip.

"Everyone have a seat," Fieldstone said.

Hurley and Naylor sat back on the couch behind them, so Sally was forced to sit beside Talon, who picked up his hat and set it on his knees. Jorge sat beside Sally, and her arm brushed against his. For some reason, she felt as if she might be blushing.

"Mr. Talon has come to us with a problem," Fieldstone said. "A somewhat serious problem."

"What problem?" Jorge asked.

"Satanism," Dr. Fieldstone said. "At least that's what Mr. Talon is calling it."

"That's not what I'm *callin'* it," Roy Don Talon said. His voice was rough but sincere, a good voice for selling cars. "That's what it *is*, plain and simple. What I want to know is, what are you-all gonna do about it?"

"It's not Satanism," Val Hurley said. "It's just a painting of a goat."

Hurley looked a little like a goat himself, Sally thought. Or a satyr. He was short, with a triangular face, and his hair, which was wavy and parted in the middle, twisted on his forehead into two hornlike curls.

"Sure it's a goat," Talon said. "And the goat is a well-known symbol of Satanism and witchcraft. You can ask anybody that knows, and they'll tell you that. And what about those numbers on his head? Huh? What about 'em?"

"Numbers?" Hurley said. "What numbers?"

"Those numbers on that goat's head. Six-six-six, plain as day. The Number of the Beast. Right out of the book of Revelations."

Sally thought about telling him that the biblical book was actually "The Revelation of St. John the Divine" and that there was no *s* on the end of the word, but she didn't. It wouldn't have done any good, and besides, Talon didn't give her a chance. He just kept right on talking.

"Don't tell me you don't know about those numbers," he

23

said. "They're right there for ever'body to see. I came out here to the art show because I like to support the college when I can, but seeing that picture gave me a shock, I'll tell you."

So that's what this was about, Sally thought. The student art show. She decided it was time to speak up.

"I didn't see any numbers," she said.

"You been to the art gallery?" Talon asked.

She said, "Yes. I go to all the exhibits."

"Did you see the picture of that goat?" Talon asked.

"Yes," Sally said, trying to remember if she actually had. If so, the painting hadn't impressed her, but she wasn't going to admit it.

"Then you've seen the numbers," Talon said. "Case closed."

Sally wasn't going to be talked to like that, even if Talon was one of the biggest taxpayers in the district. She stood up and asked, "Are you calling me a liar?"

"Now, now," Fieldstone said, standing as well. He walked out from behind his desk, the top of which was as clean as the floor of a compulsive's kitchen. Sally thought about her own desk, which by comparison looked like an explosion in a paper-recycling facility.

"No one's making any accusations," Fieldstone went on. "Mr. Talon is—"

"Mr. Talon is making accusations," Jorge said.

He didn't have to stand up to get anyone's attention. He was a commanding presence even while he was sitting down.

Talon said, "Damn right I am." He glanced at Sally. "Pardon my French, ma'am. But there's Satanism goin' on here, and I aim to put a stop to it."

"I think we should all have a look at the painting," Jorge said. "I haven't had a chance to visit the art exhibit yet."

"Very well," Fieldstone said. "You should see it before

24

forming an opinion. It was done by one of our prison students, after all."

That explained why Jorge had been asked to come to the little meeting. Val Hurley was chair of the art department, Sally was his immediate supervisor, Naylor was *her* supervisor, and Jorge oversaw the prison programs. Nothing like spreading the blame around. That way, even if the painting had something to do with black magic or Satanism, which Sally seriously doubted, none of the blame would stick to Fieldstone.

"Let's all step over to the gallery," Fieldstone said. "And have a look at the painting."

Jorge was the closest to the door, and when he opened it, Sally thought she saw Eva Dillon hastily shove what looked like the remains of a Snickers into a desk drawer. Sally gave her a thumbs-up and led the way to the gallery, which was upstairs in the Art and Music Building next door.

Jorge followed her up the stairs, and when they went through the gallery's doors, she said, "You might want to sign the guest book, Jorge. The students appreciate your support."

Jorge said nothing, but he smiled, revealing teeth almost as white as Fieldstone's. Sally had heard that dental students got part of their training by doing work in the prisons. Evidently they did a good job.

The gallery was a long, narrow room, shaped like a capital *T*. The entrance doors were at the foot of the *T,* and there was a small white pedestal to the right. The guest book sat atop it.

Jorge glanced down the length of the gallery.

"Which painting is Mr. Talon objecting to?"

Talon, who had come in behind him, said, "That one right down there."

He pointed to the end of the room, at the crossbar of the *T.* Sally looked in that direction and saw what might have

25

been a section of a goat's head in a painting that was partially concealed by the wall. She vaguely recalled having seen it on her previous visit, but she certainly didn't remember any numbers on its forehead. Of course, she wouldn't have been looking for them. Goats weren't her favorite animal.

"Let's have a closer look," Jorge said, leading the way down the narrow room.

The walls on both sides held paintings, watercolors, and drawings done in pencil, charcoal, and pen and ink. Many of them were amateurish, but a number showed real promise, or so Sally thought. However, she wasn't much of an art critic; her tastes ran to the sweeping landscapes of the Romantic era, and there was nothing like that on display. Instead, there were still lifes of fruit, some teddy bears, several portraits, and lots of cow skulls.

The middle of the room was filled with sculptures, mostly free-form, some of them ceramic, others plaster, and some made from metal that seemed to have been scavenged from a junkyard. Sally was careful not to brush them as she passed. Most of them seemed precariously balanced on their white pedestals.

When they had all gathered at the end of the gallery, Roy Don Talon stood in front of the painting of the goat and pointed in triumph.

"There it is," he said. "Plain as day—six-six-six. The Number of the Beast!"

Sally looked at the forehead of the goat. As far as she could tell, there was nothing there at all.

5

I don't see any numbers," Jorge said, leaning toward the painting. "And it doesn't even look much like a goat. It could be a buffalo, maybe."

Sally was glad to hear him say it; the animal didn't look much like a goat to her, either. It looked more like a sheep with horns.

Talon stepped forward, nudging Jorge with his shoulder. If he was trying to push Jorge aside, it didn't work. Nudging him had about as much effect as nudging a Chrysler.

"Look here," Talon said. He tapped the painting with a finger. "You mean to tell me you don't see any numbers right there?"

"Not a one," Jorge said. "All I see is hair. Or maybe it's wool. Are you sure this isn't some kind of Rocky Mountain sheep?"

A flush was spreading from the base of Talon's neck up to his ears. He said, "It's a damn goat, an imp of Satan, and those are numbers right there on its fiendish forehead!"

"It looks more as if the hair is just tangled there," Sally

said. "I don't think there are any actual patterns in it."

Talon traced the curves of the hair with his fingers. "Now then. You see? Are you going to try to tell me those aren't sixes?"

"They aren't if you look at them this way," Jorge said. He put out a hand that could have crushed Talon's like a paper cup, and traced the hairs in a different direction. "This way, it looks more like nine-one-one. It could be a subliminal suggestion to call the police. I'd call this a law-and-order painting."

Talon's eyes narrowed. "I've heard a thing or two about you, Rodriguez. You're real big about spending taxpayers' money on helping prisoners get themselves educated and 're-habilitated.' "

Sally could actually hear the quotation marks around the last word. Talon clearly didn't have a high opinion of the effects of education on prisoners.

"There have been quite a few studies done," she said. "All of them show that the one thing that reduces recidivism more than any other is education."

Talon turned his gaze on her. "I guess you think something like this picture is educational."

Sally nodded. "I do, yes. It's a good creative outlet, and it gives the men something to do with their time."

"Men?" Talon said. "You mean convicts, don't you?"

"They're still men," Jorge said.

Talon swiveled his neck and glared at Jorge, who returned the car dealer's stare with mild amusement.

"Now, now, gentlemen," Dean Naylor said calmly. "Let's not forget why we're here."

Sally had wondered when Naylor would speak up. He would be the one Fieldstone was counting on to smooth things over, and if anyone could do it, he could. He was the college's master of double-talk. Sally had once gone to his office to get the answer to what she thought was a simple yes-or-no question. When she had left an hour later, she still didn't have an answer. Not only that, but she'd forgotten the question.

"We're here about this Satanic picture, is what we're here for," Talon said.

Naylor smoothly insinuated himself into the narrow space between Talon and Jorge. Sally marveled at his skill; Naylor wasn't a small man, and she wouldn't have thought there was room for him.

"Let's examine the picture again," Naylor said. "I think we can all agree that the . . . um, *numbers* aren't really as plain as they might be."

"Maybe so, maybe not," Talon said. "But that's because the convict is trying to hide them. You can see them if you're looking. They're there all right."

"I'll tell you what we'll do," Naylor said. "And I think you'll agree that it's the right thing."

"Not unless you take down that picture, I won't," Talon said. "It doesn't belong on the wall of a college art gallery. As a taxpayer in this district, I think it's offensive."

Naylor said, "I was going to suggest that we simply have a group of our instructors come in and evaluate the picture. We'll have them come in and critique the exhibit, without giving them instructions to focus on any particular picture. If even one of them suggests that this painting of a . . . um, *goat* suggests Satanism, or finds it offensive in any way, we'll remove it from the walls at once."

Talon seemed about to launch into a criticism of this approach when Val Hurley spoke up. "I don't think that's a good idea. It's censorship of the worst kind. It's just not acceptable."

Talon said, "Now you just hold on there. That's not censorship. It's a good idea. I think ever'body will see that this is a subversive and offensive picture and that it ought to be taken down off that wall as soon as they look at it. Who's gonna be on that panel, Naylor?"

"Faculty members from several different departments," Naylor said. "I'll get a good cross section of the college."

Hurley protested again. "I don't think that's fair. I think you should pick people who are at least a little familiar with the principles of art."

"Bull corn," Talon said. "Naylor, you get some real folks in here, not a bunch of artsy-fartsy types." He looked at Sally. "Pardon my French again, ma'am. You gonna get real folks, Naylor?"

Fieldstone stepped in. "Of course we will, Mr. Talon. You don't have to worry about that. People from the business department, the nursing area, automotive repair. Maybe the welding instructor."

Talon smiled. "Sounds like a good cross section to me. I like for things to be done fair and square."

Sally had to admire the guile of Naylor, Fieldstone, and Hurley. They were playing Talon like an old fiddle. If she hadn't known better, she would have bet that Val had been rehearsed. For that matter, maybe he had.

"Why don't you come back to my office with me?" Naylor said to Talon. "I'd like to get your ideas on ways we can improve the college, if you'd be willing to share them with us. I'm sure you have some valuable suggestions."

"Well, I do have an idea or two," Talon said.

"Great!" Naylor said.

The dean slipped his arm around Talon's shoulder. That was one of the things about him that Sally didn't like. He was a touchy-feely type, and sometimes he made her uncomfortable. She had to admit that he touched both men and women, and she knew that he meant nothing by it, but it still bothered her.

Talon set his ten-gallon hat on his brush-cut hair, and Naylor led him out a door at the end of the crossbar, the two of them talking animatedly about the future of Hughes Community College, Sally supposed.

Jorge watched them go. "Another soul made happy," he said.

"He thinks he's happy now," Fieldstone said. "Later, it might be a different story."

"When the painting doesn't come down?" Sally said.

"It's a possibility." Fieldstone tugged at the knot of his tie. "But we can't afford to have people interfering with academic freedom."

"Why not just explain the concept to him?" Jorge asked.

"Why not try to explain it to this sculpture?" Val Hurley said, putting his hand on an amorphous ceramic piece.

Jorge smiled. He was handsome when he smiled, Sally thought, in a sort of gangsterish way.

"How can you be so sure the committee will give you the right evaluation?" he asked Fieldstone.

Fieldstone nodded toward the painting. "Do any of you see any numbers?"

"No," Sally said.

"Of course not," Hurley said.

"Just nine-one-one," Jorge said. "Obviously symbolic of the police state. It would be better if this were a painting of a pig, though."

Fieldstone grinned. "That's not the interpretation you gave before, but who knows? You may be right. At any rate, now it's time for all of us to get back to work. Dr. Good, I need to see you and Mr. Hurley in my office. We have something else to discuss."

What now? Sally thought. Then she remembered A. B. D. Johnson and his complaint.

"We'll be right there," she said. "I need to have a word with Val first."

Fieldstone turned to leave. "Ten minutes?"

Sally nodded. "Ten minutes."

When Fieldstone was out of earshot, Jorge said, "That was pretty slick work, Val. Did you get together with Naylor beforehand and plan it?"

"No. But I could see by the way things were going that Talon wouldn't agree unless he thought it would be to his advantage. So I just helped him think so."

"Well," Jorge said, "it was well done. If you ever want to run a con on somebody, you'll do okay."

"I don't want to con anyone," Val said. "I just want to be left alone to teach my students."

"I don't blame you," Jorge said. "That's all any of us asks for. Just time to do our jobs. Walk you back to your office, Dr. Good?"

"I have to talk to Val before we go to Fieldstone's office again."

"Right. I forgot about that. See you later, then."

Jorge left by the same door that Naylor and Talon had gone through. When it had closed behind him, Val said, "He seems like a nice guy. Did you ever hear why he was in prison?"

"He killed someone," Sally said.

"I know that. But who did he kill?"

Whom, Sally thought, but she said, "I don't know. Right now, though, we have to talk about your chair."

"My chair?"

"Your new office chair. A. B. D. Johnson is upset."

Val smiled a goatish smile. "I'm shocked."

Sally laughed. "I'll bet. Anyway, I just wanted to warn you that he's threatening to send a memo of complaint to Fieldstone. In fact, that might be why Fieldstone wants to see us.

A. B. D. might have bypassed the memo and complained in person."

"Dr. Fieldstone doesn't like complaints much, does he?" Val said.

"No. But you don't have to worry about this one. It doesn't have anything to do with you, not really. And that reminds me—did you pick the pictures to be displayed in this exhibit?"

"No. They were juried. Of course, I was on the jury with the other art instructors. I didn't like that painting, though. No one did."

"Then why is it here?"

"Because it was the only one submitted by any of our prison students. We thought it would be a nice boost for him to have it on display here."

"Too bad it didn't turn out that way," Sally said.

"Oh, it's a nice boost, no matter what Talon says. We just won't tell the artist there was any controversy."

"Good," Sally said. "And if you see A. B. D. coming, you'll know what he has to say."

"Thanks for the warning. I hope that's not what Dr. Fieldstone wants to talk to us about. I don't feel much like defending my chair to him."

"I don't blame you," Sally said. "It's probably something else."

But she didn't really think so.

6

Jack Neville was working on an article for *Golden Disc* when A. B. D. Johnson stopped by. *Golden Disc* wasn't what anyone would consider a scholarly periodical, but no one at Hughes was required to publish scholarly articles, or any other kind of articles. So Jack could write whatever he wanted to write and send it wherever he wanted to send it.

"Working on another one of those academic monographs?" asked A. B. D. "Maybe something about Bobby Rydell as an innovative stylist?"

Neville looked at Johnson, taking in his scuffed loafers, his baggy Dockers (clearly not the wrinkle-free variety), his sad face, his unruly hair. Neville didn't appreciate Johnson's sarcasm, and for a second or two he considered making some disparaging remark about Walt Whitman, particularly the Calamus poems, but he restrained himself.

He put down his pen, leaned back in his chair (not the executive model), and said, "I'm writing about Buddy Holly, if you're really interested."

"I'm not," Johnson said. His bluntness was one of the

things that Neville didn't like about him. "I came by to talk to you about your chair."

"My chair? Are you kidding me?"

"I'm not kidding. That chair's in pretty bad shape. It's ripped there on the back."

Johnson pointed, but Neville didn't bother to look. He knew the chair's shortcomings, which were many.

"So?" Neville said.

"So some of the stuffing's leaking out. And I'll bet it squeaks."

"The stuffing?" Neville asked.

"The chair."

"Oh."

Neville leaned forward. The chair squeaked.

"By George, you're right," he said. "I guess it needs a shot of WD-40."

"Val Hurley has a new chair," Johnson said. "An expensive one."

Neville shrugged and leaned squeakily back again. "Good for him."

A. B. D. shoved his hair up off his forehead. It fell right back down. "Doesn't it make you angry that some people spend money for things like chairs when the school's short of money? Hurley could just as well have used his old chair for a few more years, just like you're doing."

"Don't get all worked up about it. A chair's not that expensive."

"It's not the money," Johnson said. "It's the principle of the thing. I think it's outrageous, and I think someone should do something about it."

"Not me," Neville said. "I have to prove that Buddy Holly was a more innovative artist than Elvis."

A. B. D. Johnson snorted. "That's the trouble with this place. Nobody cares about anything important."

"You don't think Buddy Holly is important?"

"You know what I mean. Everyone has a secure little job, and we're all supposed to be happy as long as nobody rocks the boat."

"Look," Neville said. "Here's the way it is. I'm not getting rich, but I've got a good job, and I love doing it. I even get to write articles for *Golden Disc*, which I probably couldn't do if I were working for some big university. I'd have to work on serious studies of the significance of the lack of punctuation in Quentin Compson's section of *The Sound and the Fury*, or on something else that doesn't really interest me. I'd be spending the rest of my time worrying about getting tenure or complaining about having to teach composition classes just because I wouldn't be supposed to enjoy them. But I *like* teaching composition, which is what I do here. So why shouldn't I be happy and satisfied?"

A. B. D. gave him an exasperated look. "Because nothing ever changes! We need to shake things up, get some new blood in here, get a fresh start!"

"Well, you shake things up, then. I'm more interested in writing about Buddy Holly."

"Apathy!" Johnson said. His face was getting dangerously red. "That's all there is around here. No wonder this school's going to hell in a handbasket."

"I'm not apathetic," Neville said. "I'm just not excited about the same things you are. If you want things to change, get busy and change them."

"Maybe I will," Johnson said, and he stomped away down the hall.

Neville, glad to see him leave, turned back to his desk and picked up his pen. He had a computer in the office, but he preferred to write his first drafts out in longhand and then polish them up as he entered them into the computer's memory. And then there was his secret shame, which also kept

37

him from the computer and which he didn't like to think about.

So he wouldn't.

He read over the last paragraph of his article, but he couldn't get back into the flow of things. With a glance over his shoulder at the computer, he laid the pen down again. Damn that A. B. D. anyway. He was always causing trouble in the department, so much so that Jack hated going to departmental meetings. Not that Sally held many meetings. That was one of the things that Jack liked about her.

It wasn't one of the important things, however. What he liked even more was the way her smile was just a little crooked, and the little crinkles at the corners of her eyes. And the way she looked him straight in the eye when she talked to him. Not to mention the way that she looked in the tights she wore to aerobics class.

He'd seen her only by accident, of course, one late afternoon when he'd been passing by the room where the class met. Pausing for a moment to watch the exercisers was only natural, or so he told himself. He might have grown to adulthood in a less enlightened era, but that didn't mean he was a sexist pig. He hoped.

But maybe he was. It wasn't easy to get the image of Sally in the leotard out of his mind. Not that he'd tried very hard.

Sally had come to Hughes six years earlier, just after her husband had died in a car crash—an accident, Jack had heard, though Troy Beauchamp had spread the rumor that it was suicide.

"He had an inoperable tumor," Troy said. "I know a man who knows the family, and he says that Good couldn't take the pain any longer. So he ended things in a way that would look like an accident. That way Sally got the double-indemnity payment."

Jack had no idea whether Troy was telling the truth. It was always that way with Troy's stories. They were plausible, but you could never be sure about their veracity. Troy would pass along any story that he heard, no matter what the reliability of the source might be.

Anyway, whatever had happened to Sally's husband was beside the point. She was single, and that was all that interested Jack.

For her first two years at Hughes, she had kept pretty much to herself, which was all right. She was a division chair, after all. People in positions of power, even such power as a division chair had, sometimes liked to hold themselves aloof.

But then something had changed. Maybe she had finally gotten over the worst of her grief. At any rate, she began dating.

She didn't date anyone from the college, but Jack heard stories (mostly from Troy Beauchamp) about her going out with some of the more prominent members of the community and even with an administrator or two from colleges in Houston.

He didn't blame her. She needed to get out, have a little fun. Jack didn't get out himself, but he could certainly understand someone who did.

Jack had been married, too, but not for long. His wife had left him while he was still in graduate school, saying that he was paying more attention to his studies than to her. She had probably been right, and Jack was sorry that he hadn't arranged his priorities differently. It was too late for that now, however, and he'd never really thought about getting married again.

Oh, he'd dated a lot of different women, and unlike Sally, he hadn't restricted himself to people outside the college community. There were still a couple of women on the faculty and staff who held grudges against him because they thought he'd led them on. And, like his wife, they were probably right.

Still, he didn't think his breaking up with them had been all his fault. None of them had been exactly perfect. Vera Vaughn, for example. Holy smoke! Troy Beauchamp occasionally liked to speculate about her sex life. If he only knew.

Jack knew, and he suspected that Val Hurley knew. Val had dated Vera only recently, and while they appeared physically mismatched—Vera tall and lithe, Val short and stocky—they might have been better matched than they appeared. Jack had always thought Val looked a little like a satyr. Whatever the case, Vera and Val were no longer going together. Jack had no idea why. Maybe he could ask Troy.

Jack shook his head and tried to drag his mind back to Buddy Holly and the article he was writing. It was impossible. The trouble was that he was very attracted to Sally Good, and that no doubt proved something perverse about him. He was sure that she was never going to date anyone from the college, and even if she did, it wouldn't be him.

He thought about the great teenage confidence that Buddy Holly expressed in songs like "That'll Be the Day" and "Not Fade Away." Too bad I don't have confidence like that, Jack thought. But then I'm not sixteen anymore.

A little voice in his head said, *You didn't have confidence like that even when you were sixteen.*

"Oh, shut up," Jack said.

7

———————

I'm sorry to take up more of your time," Fieldstone said. "But we have a serious matter to settle."

He was sitting behind his big desk again, with Sally and Val on the couch opposite him. He looked too serious to be talking about something like an office chair, and Sally wondered what was going on. Maybe he was talking about the painting again.

"I thought we'd just settled things," she said. "Mr. Talon seems satisfied with the solution Dean Naylor offered."

"I'm not talking about the painting," Fieldstone said. "The goat's nothing. This is different, and much more serious."

Sally had no idea what was going on, and it was clear from his expression that Val didn't either. So Sally decided to take the risk of looking foolish.

"Is it about Val's new chair?"

Fieldstone sat up a little straighter. "New chair? What new chair? Are you joking, Dr. Good?"

Well, she'd known she might look foolish.

"No, I'm not joking," she said. "It's just that A. B. D.—I

mean, Perry—Johnson came by my office today to complain that Val had bought a new office chair. I thought maybe Perry had come by to complain to you, too."

"No," Fieldstone said. "And he'd better not. Let him put his thoughts in a memo if he wants to complain. I don't have time to deal with petty departmental jealousies."

To her mild surprise, Sally found herself defending A. B. D. "This isn't petty, not to A. B.—to Perry. He thinks we shouldn't be spending the college's money on luxuries like new office chairs."

Fieldstone assumed a lecturing manner. "Let me explain something, Dr. Good. Each department chair here at Hughes is in charge of his or her own budget. That means if Mr. Hurley"—he inclined his head toward Val—"wants to buy a chair, he can buy a chair. All he has to do is keep within his budget for the year. We may be in a mild financial bind, but we're not broke, not by a long way."

"That's what I told Perry," Sally said.

"Good. Then he doesn't need to bother me with a memo, does he?" Fieldstone didn't wait for her to answer the question. He answered it himself. "Of course he doesn't. Now about this other thing . . ."

His voice trailed off, and he looked over Sally's head and out the floor-to-ceiling window. Sally didn't have to turn around to know there wasn't anything special to see out there, not unless you had an inordinate fondness for parking lots filled with cars. She realized that Fieldstone was having difficulty broaching the subject. It must really be serious.

She sneaked another look at Val, who gave a surreptitious shrug. Finally, Fieldstone lowered his eyes to Val.

"Do you know a student named Tammi Thompson?" he asked.

Tammi had been in Sally's composition class. She was a

very pretty young woman, with beautiful long black hair and a striking figure.

"I know her," Val said. "She's in my Painting I class."

"And that's all? You don't have any other relationship with her?"

A silent warning went off in Sally's head, and Val twisted on the couch as if his underwear had suddenly shrunk three or four sizes.

"Well?" Fieldstone said.

"Well," Val said.

A saying of her grandfather's echoed through Sally's head: *Well, well. It's a deep subject for shallow minds.*

"I'm giving you an opportunity to explain, Mr. Hurley," Fieldstone said.

"There's nothing to explain, really," Val replied, but his tone indicated to Sally that there was a lot to explain. More, in fact, than Val was willing to discuss.

"I think there *is* something to explain," Fieldstone said. "I had hoped that there wouldn't be, but your behavior is making it obvious that there is. I've already heard one side of the story. Now I'm ready to listen to yours."

Sally wished that Jorge were there. He would have enjoyed the way Fieldstone was manipulating Val by withholding crucial information and giving Val every chance to hang himself.

Which he proceeded to do.

"She asked me to paint her," he said. "I didn't want to do it! She practically begged me!"

Sally groaned. Both men looked at her.

"Are you all right, Dr. Good?" Fieldstone asked.

"Yes. I'm sorry. It's just that—"

"I know," Fieldstone said. "You were surprised. So was I, when I heard about this. And I don't like surprises. Especially not this kind."

Sally told herself to get a grip. Val was one of her division

43

members, after all. It was one thing to manipulate an outsider like Talon, but she was tired of Fieldstone doing it to Val.

"Just exactly what kind of surprise was it?" she asked. "You haven't told us that."

"I thought that maybe Mr. Hurley would tell us."

"I'd rather hear what you were told," Sally said. "And I'd like to know who told you."

Fieldstone put his hands on top of the desk and steepled his fingers. Sally could see his class ring from Texas A&M. Besides surprises, another thing he didn't like was Aggie jokes.

"All right," he said. "Tammi Thompson told me."

"What did she tell you?" Val asked.

"That you were doing a painting of her."

"She asked me to."

"In the nude," Fieldstone said.

Val sank against the back of the couch.

"Is that true?" Fieldstone asked.

Val didn't say anything, and Sally groaned again, inwardly this time. She'd known from the moment Val had admitted that he was doing the painting where this was headed, and she was afraid that it was only going to get worse.

"Well?" Fieldstone asked.

"Well," Val said.

Déjà vu, Sally thought.

"It's true, isn't it?" Fieldstone said. "You're doing a painting of her in the nude."

Val nodded. "It's true."

Sally began coughing. She opened her purse and felt around inside it for a tissue. Fieldstone sighed and folded his arms across his chest.

"But she asked me to," Val said weakly. "It wasn't my idea."

"You're aware of the policy in the faculty manual, the one dealing with relationships between faculty and students?"

Val said that he was.

"Then you know that you should never have entered into a private intimate relationship with a student, no matter whose idea it might have been."

"I know, I know," Val said. "But I didn't see any real harm in it."

"Because it was her idea," Fieldstone said. "Fine. And whose idea was it for you to touch her?"

Sally put the wadded tissue back in her purse. *My God*, she thought. It was hard to believe that she'd been worried about something as silly as a new chair. Or a Satanic painting, for that matter.

"I didn't touch her," Val said. "Not really."

" 'Not really'?" Fieldstone said. "How can you 'not really' touch someone?"

"I might have touched her, but if I did, it was an accident that happened in passing. There was nothing more to it than that."

"That's not what Ms. Thompson and her husband say."

"Her husband?" Val said. "He's the reason she wanted the painting. It was going to be a gift for him. She assured me that she had cleared it with him. I wasn't worried about him at all."

"Obviously." Fieldstone's voice was cold. "And I'm sure you weren't thinking about him when you touched Ms. Thompson in an artistic way."

"I wasn't thinking of anything," Val said. "Except of course the artistic arrangement of the model."

"You sound as if you really believe that," Fieldstone said.

"I do. I know it was wrong to do the painting, but Tammi—Ms. Thompson—seemed to want it so much. She said that it would be a surprise for her husband on their anniversary."

Sally was feeling better about things. Val sounded completely sincere. Maybe he was innocent.

"A nude picture for an anniversary gift?" Fieldstone said. "Really, Mr. Hurley."

It didn't make much sense, Sally had to admit. She stopped feeling better.

"She wasn't completely nude," Val said. "She was draped."

"But of course under the drape she was nude."

"That's right. But there was nothing vulgar about it."

"So you say," Fieldstone said. "But both Ms. Thompson and her husband are quite upset. They're considering pressing charges against you. And against the school."

Sally felt almost sorry for Fieldstone. The most frightening word to any college administrator these days was *lawsuit*. Combined with a falling enrollment and financial problems, a lawsuit could prove a nearly crippling blow to the school.

Val sat forward on the couch. "But that's ridiculous. I did nothing that anyone could find offensive. I swear it."

"You might have to swear it," Fieldstone said. "In a court of law."

"I think Val and I should hear what Ms. Thompson and her husband have to say about this," Sally said. "It's only right that Val have a chance to hear their story and tell them his side of things."

"I'll see if I can arrange that," Fieldstone said. "Mr. Hurley, are you sure that Ms. Thompson made no comment to you about your actions at any time during her last sitting?"

"I'm absolutely sure. She seemed very pleased with the way things were going."

"I see. And she never objected to your fondling her?"

"I object to that word," Sally said. "You're acting as if Val has been proven guilty."

To Sally's surprise, Fieldstone said, "You're right. This isn't something for me to make a judgment on without a thorough investigation. As Mr. Hurley's immediate superior, you will have to talk to the Thompsons and bring them together with Mr. Hurley."

Sally had been afraid that he might suggest something like that. "May I ask Dean Naylor to assist me?"

"That might be a good idea," Fieldstone said.

Sally certainly thought so. Naylor was as slick as ice, and he would be able to deal with the Thompsons and Val in a way that would make both sides feel better about things.

"I'd suggest that you meet as soon as possible," Fieldstone said.

He opened a desk drawer and took out a piece of paper. Sally could see that there was something typed on it, and Fieldstone looked at it for a few seconds before handing it to her.

"Here are the Thompsons' phone number and address," he said. "Give them a call as soon as possible."

"I can't believe this is happening," Val said. "I just can't believe it."

Fieldstone leaned back in his chair and crossed his arms.

"You'd better," he said.

8

Sally went back to her office and closed the door. She sat at her cluttered desk and tried to think about the composition papers that she had to grade, but she knew that she wouldn't be grading any more of them that day. She would never be able to concentrate.

She had spent a few minutes with Val after they'd left Fieldstone's office, and he'd pleaded with her to believe in his innocence.

"I know it was wrong to do the painting," he said. "But I did nothing anything else that was wrong. I never touched Ms. Thompson in a lewd way. I never even thought about doing a thing like that. If she says I did, she's lying."

"Why would she lie about something like that, Val?" Sally asked.

Val's shoulders slumped. "I don't know. I can't understand it. She seemed so happy to be doing this for her husband, and now she's accusing me of something I didn't do. Surely you know me well enough to know I'd never do a thing like that."

Sally wanted to reassure him, but she couldn't. She'd heard that he had been dating Vera Vaughn recently, and she had the feeling that anyone who dated Vera would do just about anything.

But that was a truly uncharitable thought, and she regretted having it. To make amends, she said, "I hope that you wouldn't, Val. Maybe it's just some kind of misunderstanding."

She didn't really believe this, but it was the only thing she could think of that might make Val feel a little better.

"Whatever happened," she said, "we'll get to the bottom of it."

And speaking of bottoms, she wondered uncharitably just exactly where Val had touched Tammi. She didn't know how to ask him, however. It was a hard question to put delicately. What could she say? Somehow, "Did you grab her ass, Val?" didn't seem properly genteel.

So what she said was, "I hope that when Tammi and her husband come up for their meeting with us, we find out that there's just been some kind of communications breakdown."

"That must be it," Val said. "It has to be. A communications breakdown. A misunderstanding. That's it, all right. Tammi—Ms. Thompson—must have misinterpreted something I did, though I don't see how. Anyway, we'll get it all straightened out when we talk to her. I'm sure of it."

He hadn't *sounded* sure, Sally thought, sitting at her desk and staring at the disarray that covered it. Well, in a situation like this, there was only one thing to do.

She'd go home and get her pistol.

Hughes Community College was located at the intersection of Texas Highways 6 and 288, just a few miles from downtown Houston. The town of Hughes stretched up and down both highways in all four directions from the intersection, and most of the faculty lived near the campus. When Sally reached her red Acura Integra in the parking lot, she was only five minutes from her front door. Four if she was in a hurry.

One reason for the college's financial difficulties was that Houston had not grown in the direction everyone had anticipated. Highway 288 had seemed like a natural corridor for growth, especially after it had been widened in the late 1980s. But Houston had expanded in every direction except toward Hughes. Some in the town regarded this as a blessing, but not those involved with the college, which desperately needed to expand its tax base to keep up with its ever-increasing costs.

And, of course, one reason why Fieldstone wanted to avoid a lawsuit was that a juicy scandal, especially one involving improper conduct with a student, would cause many of Hughes's conservative parents to see to it that their sons and daughters went to some other school, causing an immediate drop in enrollment at Hughes.

To Sally's way of thinking, there were all too many other schools in the area, making it too easy for students to get an education elsewhere. Community-college extension campuses were springing up everywhere in the schools' attempts to increase their enrollment and, by doing so, to get more state funding. Just a short drive from Hughes would take students to college classes in Alvin, Brazosport, Sugar Land, Houston, Galveston, or Texas City.

So Sally understood Fieldstone's desire to get Val's case settled. Even something like the painting of the goat, as ridiculous as the idea of its Satanic implications seemed to Sally, could cause trouble.

She turned the Integra into her driveway and punched the garage-door opener. The door slid up with an annoying metallic squeal, which Sally was sure meant that the foundation of her house was shifting, a common problem in the area and one that sometimes resulted in the need for expensive repairs.

She hoped that she could avoid both the repairs and the expense because she had other expenses to worry about. The house needed a new roof, and a fresh coat of paint wouldn't hurt it, either. And new carpet would be nice.

She got out of the car and went inside the house, where she was greeted by Lola, the meanest cat west of the Mississippi—and possibly east of the Mississippi as well. Lola was a large calico, three years old, and possessed of all the charm of Attila the Hun.

Most cats liked to be rubbed and petted. Not Lola. She seemed to resent any attempt to touch her and would snarl and snap at anyone who tried, except Sally, and even Sally could get close only on rare occasions.

This wasn't one of them. As soon as Lola saw Sally come through the door, she hissed and ran through the breakfast area into the den, where she scooted under a lamp table and hid.

Sally opened a cabinet and took out a box of kitty treats. When Sally shook the box, Lola slipped out from beneath the table and zoomed back to Sally at something only slightly slower than the speed of light. While she didn't relate well to people, Lola had never met a kitty treat she didn't like.

Sally tossed a treat into the air. Lola caught it on the fly, and then settled to the floor to crunch on it.

"I hope you enjoy it," Sally said. "It's your limit for the day."

Another thing about Lola was that she was, in Sally's words, "slightly overweight." The vet had put it differently at Lola's last checkup and had given Sally a pamphlet about the dangers facing overweight pets.

"You have to put your cat on a diet," the vet told Sally. "It's for her own good."

Sally had tried her best, but Lola could be very demanding where food was concerned. In six weeks, she had lost perhaps a pound, which was good news. But her disposition had not improved.

Sally went into her bedroom and opened the top middle drawer of her dresser. Where other women might have kept nightgowns or slinky underwear, she kept a burgundy carrying case that held a Smith & Wesson Model 36, the Ladysmith. It had a three-inch barrel and rosewood grips.

Lola, having devoured her treat and for once deciding to be sociable, followed Sally into the room. She stood on her hind legs and put her front legs on the drawer, stretching her neck as she tried to see inside.

"Get down," Sally said. "This is none of your business."

She slid the drawer closed, and Lola lowered her front legs to the floor, gave Sally a disgusted look, and left the room, probably to shred the furniture or claw a hole in the already worn carpeting.

Sally put the gun case on top of the dresser and opened it. The pistol was there, looking rigidly lethal and smelling of gun oil. Sally closed the case and went into the kitchen, where she opened a can of tuna. It was dolphin-free, according to the label, though she supposed you could never be sure.

The sound of the can opener brought Lola running, and the smell of the tuna excited her so much that she actually rubbed against Sally's ankles and purred.

"All right," Sally said, "but just a little."

She gave Lola some of the tuna in a blue plastic bowl, and ate some herself, on lettuce.

She rinsed off her plate and put it in the dishwasher; then she went and got the pistol.

"See you later, Lo," she said as she left.

Lola, who was stretched out on a throw rug by the table, didn't bother to answer.

9

Sally parked in one of the faculty spaces by the Law Enforcement Building and went through a heavy steel door in the side of the building away from the classrooms. The door led into the firing range.

Several years earlier, Sally had taken a handgun safety course, more or less on a whim, and had discovered that not only was she a naturally good shot but she also liked guns.

She had never owned a gun, and she had not come from a family of gun owners. In fact, before taking the course, she had never fired a pistol or a rifle in her life. She still hadn't fired a rifle, but she had become skilled with a pistol.

At first, she had simply rented one of the pistols available at the range, but after a while she had decided that she wanted to own her own gun. The Ladysmith, which was supposedly small and light and built for a woman, actually weighed only about half an ounce less than the Chief's Special, but the grips seemed to fit her hand better and she liked the rosewood. So she bought the Ladysmith.

With the three-inch barrel, it was a little more accurate at a distance than the same gun with the two-inch barrel was, but it still wasn't exactly a target pistol. That didn't bother Sally, who wasn't interested in competition shooting. Not yet, at any rate. She was perfectly happy to be blasting away at the sinister outline on the paper targets controlled by the rangemaster. It was a wonderful way to relieve the frustrations of a hard day, even better than her aerobics class.

The only other person on the range when Sally arrived was the rangemaster for the day, Sergeant Tom Clancey. That was one reason she liked going in right after lunch. There was usually no one there at that time.

Clancey was one of the young officers employed by Campus Security. He greeted Sally with a wave and a smile.

Sally got her shooting glasses and ear protection from a small locker, put on the glasses, and fitted the earmufflike plastic coverings over her head. Then she got her pistol out of its case and took up her position on the firing line. Clancey put the target through its paces, running it from the back of the range toward her, flipping it from side to front, running it backward, and stopping it at five, ten, fifteen, and twenty-five yards.

Sally blasted away, five shots at a time. Each time she reloaded, she was careful to observe range etiquette even though no one else was around. She believed in the virtues of discipline.

When she was through shooting, a thin haze of smoke hung in the air, and Sally could smell the sharp odor of cordite. She took off her ear protection, and Sergeant Clancey ran the target up for her to examine. He came out of the booth for a look as well.

All the holes were in the black, most of them clustered in the area of the chest, though a few of them strayed toward the head and stomach.

"You should hang that on your garage door," Sergeant

Clancey said. "The burglars would give your place a wide berth."

"I don't think I could shoot a burglar if one ever showed up," Sally said.

"That's why you hang up the target. Discourage them so you won't have to shoot them."

"I don't think so," Sally said. "Just put it in the recycling box."

She went to the booth to put her pistol back in the case.

"You might be surprised what you could do if you did have someone break into your house," Sergeant Clancey said. "You're a really good shot."

"At a target. You never know what you'll do in a life-or-death situation until you face it."

Sally and Clancey both knew she was simply repeating what she had heard in her firearms class. She had also heard that if you ever fired a pistol at an intruder, you should shoot to kill. Wounding wasn't an option. She hoped never to find herself in that situation.

"You sure you don't want the target for a souvenir?" Sergeant Clancey asked as she was leaving.

"No, thanks," she said.

Back in her office, Sally called the number Fieldstone had given her for the Thompsons. She got an answering machine with a supposedly humorous tape that Sally didn't find at all funny. She wondered why people didn't just record their own announcements, and she thought about not leaving a message at all. In the end, however, she left both her office and home numbers and asked the Thompsons to call.

She spent the rest of the afternoon grading compositions, and she was proud of herself for finishing all those for her Friday class. She could return them the next day and spend the class period analyzing them with the students. She went to the workroom to make transparencies of several papers that she wanted to use for illustrative purposes.

The workroom was almost as deserted as the firing range. After all, it was nearly four o'clock. Few of the faculty stayed around much past three or three-thirty unless they had evening classes. Today, the only other person around was Merle Menton, the chair of the Division of Social Sciences, who was reading a newspaper in the lounge, which adjoined the workroom.

Though Merle was nearing retirement age, he still had a full head of very black hair, hair that was the object of much speculation by the rest of the Hughes faculty. Did he dye it or not?

Troy Beauchamp's answer was a definite yes. He swore that he had talked to someone who had seen Menton buying a package of Just for Men at the local Wal-Mart, but there were several who weren't convinced by his story.

Sally was one of them. Menton's hair just didn't look dyed, and what difference did it make if it was? What bothered her about Menton was his personality, which bordered on the terminally dull. He could talk endlessly in his bland, monotonous baritone about almost any subject that popped into his head, and he would continue for as long he could get anyone to listen. Or force them to listen. His favorite technique was to back the reluctant listener into a corner and stand so that there was no escape short of death.

When Sally saw him, she was careful to stand on the side of the transparency maker that was farthest from the corner, which was a good thing. When he heard the machine begin to operate, Menton stood up and began to sidle toward her.

"I'm waiting for my wife to come pick me up," he said as he approached. "My car is in the shop."

There was a faculty legend that Menton had once trapped a part-time instructor in the lounge and talked nonstop for six hours about the time the timing chain went out on his 1983 Buick. Sally didn't want something like that to happen, so she grabbed the last transparency as it fed from the machine and started toward the door.

"I have a student waiting in the office," she lied brazenly and unashamedly. "Otherwise, I'd love to hear about your car. What seems to be the trouble?"

"It's the transmission," Menton droned. "I had the fluid checked last week, but it seems to have all run out in the road as I drove to school yesterday. I hope the transmission's not burned up. I've heard—"

"I'm sure it's fine," Sally said, not sure at all. She didn't know a thing about transmissions. "You can tell me about it sometime when I don't have a student waiting."

She made her escape, feeling slightly guilty about the disappointment on Menton's face as she'd gone through the door. Thank goodness he hadn't gotten her into a corner. She might have missed her aerobics class.

On her way back to her office, she passed Jack Neville's door. It was closed, but there was a light showing underneath it. She wondered if he were still working or if he had left the light on by accident. She knocked on the door.

There was no answer. It didn't matter that the light was on. One of the cleaning crew would turn it off later. Then she thought she heard something that sounded like the squeak of an office chair. She knocked again.

Jack Neville opened the door.

"Oh," he said. He seemed surprised to see her. "Hi."

"Hi," she said. "Working late?"

Jack looked over his shoulder at the computer, which was turned on. Nothing was visible on the screen except the main menu, however.

"Just doing a little work on an article," he said.

"For that record magazine?"

"That's the one."

"What's the article about?"

"Buddy Holly and Elvis Presley," Jack said. "I guess you're a little young to have been a fan when you were growing up."

"I'm more of a Creedence Clearwater Revival fan."

"They were good, all right," Jack said. "Uh, would you like to come in and sit down?"

Jack's office was much smaller than Sally's and not a lot neater, but he had a chair for visitors beside his desk.

"I wish I could," Sally said. "But I have an aerobics class in just a few minutes. I have to go change and get ready."

"Oh," Jack said, his ears reddening.

Sally wondered why, but didn't mention it. "I hope you get the article done. I'd like to read it."

"I'll give you a copy when it's finished."

"See you tomorrow, then," Sally said, and went on down the hall.

When she turned the corner to her own office, she wondered why she always seemed to feel awkward when she talked to Jack. He was certainly nice enough, and an excellent instructor. And he was good-looking in a sort of rumpled manner. Not as overtly macho as Jorge, but just as attractive in his own shy way.

But she shouldn't be thinking of either of them in this way, she told herself. She'd promised herself when she came to Hughes that there would be no involvements with men at the school. Involvement could lead to complications—just look at Val Hurley.

Of course, Val's involvement was with a student, and that *always* led to complications. She wondered what had come over Val that would lead him to do a painting of a student. She didn't really know him very well; their relationship, like

60

all her relationships with school personnel, was strictly professional.

She'd heard, mainly from Troy Beauchamp, that Val was quite a romantic sort. He wasn't Sally's type, but he was apparently considered attractive by a number of the single women on the faculty. He should never have allowed himself to get into his current situation.

But he *had* allowed himself, and now it was her problem almost as much as his. She went back to her office to see if there was a message from the Thompsons on her machine.

10

Jack Neville sat in his squeaky chair and stared at his computer screen. He wished he hadn't been so ill at ease when Sally had come to his door, but it was too late to worry about that now. At least he'd exited the game before he'd answered the door.

The game, something called Minesweeper, had come packaged with his computer software, and his secret shame was that he was addicted to it.

It was infuriatingly simple, not to mention simpleminded, and it bothered Jack that he couldn't seem to stop playing it. He'd never thought of himself as having an addictive personality before.

After all, he'd quit smoking fifteen years previously without so much as a single day's withdrawal symptoms. Sure, he occasionally still dreamed about smoking, but he hadn't had a cigarette in all that time.

And when he'd started getting jittery every day about three o'clock and decided the cause might just be the dozen cups of coffee he'd drunk by that time of day, he'd cut back to a single cup a day, in the morning, without thinking twice. Well, he might have thought twice, but he'd done it without agonizing about it.

So why couldn't he quit playing the blasted game?

That was the main reason why he was working on his manuscript in longhand. He didn't dare turn on the computer for fear that he'd never get a single word written. He'd spend all his time trying to put the little flags in the right squares.

He'd turned on the computer at about one o'clock to start entering his article, but he hadn't entered a word. He'd played the stupid game for three hours instead. Now it was past time to go home, and he hadn't accomplished a thing all afternoon. Well, he'd do better tomorrow.

He turned off the computer and left his handwritten article on the desk. Maybe he could get Wynona Reed, the division's secretary, to type it for him. It was a legitimate request, he thought, even if it couldn't exactly be considered an academic publication.

He picked up a stack of American literature exams. He'd punish himself by grading them at home.

Sally changed for the aerobics class in her office. It was easier than going home, even though she lived so close. She could lock the door and have all the privacy she needed. She kept a gym bag under her desk, and the change didn't take long at all. After class, she could drive home for a shower.

The class was held in the choir room rather than the gym because the choir room was large enough for the class and there was a sound system already set up there. The choir director wasn't fond of having his room used for what he referred to as a "sweaty exercise ritual" every Tuesday and Thursday afternoon, but Dean Naylor had brushed his protests aside.

The class was open to both men and women, but there

were no men enrolled. Most of the women were there to get one hour's credit toward the school's two-hour physical education requirement. The men generally took bowling or weight training, but everyone had to take something. The administration at Hughes believed that sound minds and sound bodies went together.

So did Sally, sort of. At any rate, she believed it enough to put in an enthusiastic eighty minutes or so twice a week, working out to sterile instrumental versions of old rock songs. She liked to think that the occasional Hershey bars were just melting right out of her system with every step she took, and whether or not this was true, it made her feel good to think so. She seldom missed a class.

After changing, she pulled her office door shut and stepped into the hall, practically bumping into Jack Neville.

"Ah, I'm sorry," he said. "I, ah, didn't see you coming out of your office. I guess I was thinking about these exams."

He held up the sheaf of papers that he was carrying in his right hand.

Sally smiled. "That's all right. I didn't see you, either. I'm on my way to aerobics class."

"I, ah, see that you are. Those are nice, ah, leotards."

Jack was blushing, but Sally didn't mind. It was nice to know that she could still have that effect on a man. She found herself wondering how Jorge would react in the same situation. Not like Jack, she decided.

Jack walked down the hall beside her. "Don't stop in the lounge," he warned. "I saw Dr. Menton go in there earlier."

"I've already seen him," Sally said. "He's got transmission problems."

"How did you escape?"

"I lied."

"Good idea."

They walked in silence after that until they got outside.

The sun was getting low, but there was never much of a sunset in Hughes. Or if there was, it couldn't be seen. The land was too flat, and there were too many houses in the way. But the sky was darkening, and the warmth of the day was beginning to give way to the comparative chill of the evening.

"I'm going over to the Art and Music Building," Sally said.

"I know," Jack said. "I mean, I know that's where the aerobics classes are held. Not that I've ever been by there. It's printed in the schedule."

He was talking too fast, and Sally stopped to look at him. "Why, Jack," she said. "You're getting red."

"It's this evening air," he said. "I've got to get on my way now. Lots of papers to grade."

He brandished the stack of papers again and fled the scene. Sally smiled as he trotted away.

Jack tossed the exams onto the seat of his three-year-old Corolla, got in, and closed the door. He certainly had handled that well, he told himself. About as well as the average fourteen-year-old, probably, if the fourteen-year-old was particularly socially inept.

He decided that he needed a drink, so instead of going home, he drove to the Seahorse Club. There were no bars as such in Hughes. Some places sold beer, but hard liquor was available only in "private clubs." There were several clubs, and all of them had extremely low membership fees. The one preferred by most of the Hughes faculty was the Seahorse, mainly because it was near the campus.

When Jack went inside, he blinked his eyes to let them adjust to the dim light. After a second or so, he thought he saw Jorge Rodriguez and Vera Vaughn in a semiprivate booth in the back, but while Jack was still blinking, Troy Beauchamp beckoned from a nearby table where he was sitting with Samuel Winston.

Winston had an owl-like stare and a bad attitude. Jack wasn't sure what caused the stare, but the attitude was the result of the fact that Winston was teaching at a backwater community college in Texas rather than at Harvard, which was where he'd thought he'd wind up after his distinguished academic career. Harvard hadn't been hiring, however, and neither had most of the other four-year institutions in the country. Or maybe Winston's record wasn't as sterling as he led people to believe. At any rate, he'd taken a job at Hughes and never left.

Jack wasn't especially fond of either Beauchamp or Winston, but he went over to the table.

"Hey, Jack," Beauchamp said. "Have a seat."

Winston wasn't as enthusiastic, but he didn't object, so Jack sat down.

"Gin and tonic," Beauchamp said, raising his glass. "Keeps down the incidence of malaria. What are you having?"

"Gin and tonic sounds good."

A young blond waitress walked over and took his order. Jack knew that to be politically correct he should think of her as a *server*, but his mind just didn't work that way. He was trying to change, however.

"Heard about Val Hurley?" Troy asked when the waitress was gone.

"No, what about him?"

"Big trouble," Winston said, shaking his head.

Samuel Winston was a pedantic sort. No one ever called him Sam. Most afternoons, he could be found at the Seahorse, moistening his sorrows. He never even came close to drowning them.

The waitress came back and put Jack's drink down on a little white napkin.

"Put it on my tab," Troy said.

Jack knew this meant that Troy would be assessing him

when it was time to leave. Troy always volunteered to run a tab, and Jack, who wasn't very good at math, had an uncomfortable suspicion that Troy generally made a slight profit from his friends.

The waitress smiled and asked if Troy and Samuel wanted their drinks freshened. They didn't.

Jack took a sip of the gin and tonic and said, "So what kind of trouble is Val Hurley in?"

"Aside from the Satanism?" Troy asked.

Jack took another sip, a much bigger one this time. "Maybe you'd better start at the beginning," he said. "And tell me all about it."

11

The next morning at quarter after nine, Sally was in her office speaking to Dean Naylor on the telephone, explaining to him that she hadn't been able to reach the Thompsons.

"I left a message yesterday afternoon," she said. "And I called again last night from home. The machine picked up again, so I left another message. But they haven't returned my calls."

"Call them again, right now," Naylor said. "Dr. Fieldstone wants us to meet with them as soon as possible. In fact, he was hoping that we'd have a meeting set up for this morning."

"I'll see what I can do," Sally told him. "But if they won't answer the phone or respond to my messages, I don't know what we can do about it."

"We'd better do *something*," Naylor said. "This is a very serious situation, and Dr. Fieldstone wants it resolved at once."

Sally hung up and sat for a moment, quietly fuming. She sensed that Naylor was somehow blaming her for the Thompsons' failure to get back to her, and she didn't like it. But it probably wasn't Naylor's fault. He was under pressure from Fieldstone.

She picked up the phone and had started to dial the Thompsons' number when a student appeared at her office door. He stood there looking at her expectantly, so she hung up the phone and asked if she could help him.

"I guess so. You're Dr. Good, right?"

He was a skinny young man, about twenty, with a vacant look and a baseball cap that he wore backward, a custom that Sally couldn't quite figure out. Did having the bill pointed in the wrong direction somehow help water drain off the cap better in the not infrequent rainstorms that visited the area? she wondered.

"Yes, I'm Dr. Good," she said. "What can I do for you?"

"Well, I'm in Mr. Hurley's nine o'clock class, and he hasn't shown up. Some of us thought maybe he was sick, but no one has come to let us know. I figured that since you were the division chair, you'd know whether the class was cancelled."

Sally didn't know. She was supposed to, however. Faculty members were required to notify their department chairs when they were going to be absent, and of course the department chair would notify the head of his or her division.

Sally looked at her watch. It was nearly nine-twenty. Val had never been more than a few minutes late for his classes. She thought it might be a good idea to go over to the Art and Music Building.

"What class is it?" she asked.

"Art Appreciation."

That meant a fairly sizable class. Lots of students took Art Appreciation to satisfy part of their core-curriculum requirements.

"Is the rest of the class waiting?" she asked.

"Yeah. Some of 'em left, but most of 'em are still there. Mr. Hurley doesn't like absences."

"Let's walk over there, then. If Mr. Hurley's not there when we get there, I'll have everyone sign a roll sheet and give it to him. He's probably had car trouble."

She hoped that was all it was. These days, nearly everyone had a cellular phone, and she was sure that Val was no different. Even if he'd had trouble on the road, he could have called to let her know he'd be late.

She walked over to the Art and Music Building with the student trailing along behind. The classrooms were on the second floor, beside the art gallery, and when she got there, the lecture room was partially filled with students who were talking, reading, laughing, and probably not thinking very much about art. Val Hurley was nowhere to be seen.

Sally went to the front of the room and announced that it seemed Mr. Hurley was going to be late. Several of the students groaned aloud.

"I can't believe I got up and drove over here for this," said a young man in the front row. "This is my only class until noon. I coulda slept three more hours."

"I'm sorry for the inconvenience," Sally said. She looked in the desk and found a sheet of notebook paper. "I'll pass around this paper for you to sign so Mr. Hurley will know you made the effort to be here in case he can't make it."

"More of an effort than he did," said the boy in the front row. "That's for sure."

Sally let it go. She didn't like it when faculty members had to miss class without notice, especially ones like Val, who put such an emphasis on student attendance. In his Art Appreciation classes, he even tied attendance to the final grade.

The students began gathering up their books as soon as they'd signed the roll. Sally couldn't understand why Val, who was already in trouble, would do something that would upset her and everyone in the administration who found out about it. Not that she would report him. She was used to covering for her faculty.

After everyone had signed the roll, Sally folded the paper and put it in her purse. She'd drop it in the faculty mail for Val later. She left the classroom and went out through the gallery, pausing this time to look again at some of the pictures. That was when she noticed that one of them was missing.

The one of the goat.

She suddenly got a hollow feeling in her stomach. Val was missing and so was the painting. There was something ominous about that.

The art offices were at the base of the T-shaped gallery, on either side of the entrance to one of the studios. There were only two offices because Hughes had a small art faculty. Very small, in fact. Val was the only full-time member of the department. He hired part-time instructors to teach the rest of the classes.

Sally walked the length of the gallery and knocked on Val's door. There was no answer, so she tried the knob. The door was locked, as she'd expected, but she saw Angelina Sanchez, one of the maintenance crew, in the hallway mopping up a spill. She asked Angelina to come in and open the office door.

And that was how she and Angelina came to discover the body of the late Val Hurley.

12

Jack Neville had come to take a look at the student art exhibit and was signing his name in the visitors' register when he heard Sally's voice coming from Val Hurley's office. Curious, Jack stepped around the corner and looked into the office.

Sally was talking to someone on the phone, but it wasn't Val Hurley. Val was lying on the floor, right beside his brand new chair. Straddling him was Angelina Sanchez, attempting to administer CPR.

Jack's first thought was that Val must have had a heart attack, though Jack wouldn't have considered Val a prime candidate for such a fate. Val was very careful about his diet, didn't smoke, and—aside from his current dalliance with Vera Vaughn—didn't take any unnecessary chances with his health.

Jack was about to say something when he saw a statuette of *Winged Victory* lying on the floor not far from Val's head. There was something that looked a lot like blood on the base of the statuette, and there was blood in Val's hair. Jack was no Sherlock Holmes, but he was suddenly pretty sure that Val's current situation wasn't due to any health-related problems.

Sally set the phone in its cradle and immediately picked it up again. Jack watched her punch in a 9 for an outside line and then 9-1-1. He listened as she told the dispatcher where to send the ambulance and the police.

Jack knelt down next to Val and felt his neck, trying to locate one of the carotid arteries. There was no pulse, not the faintest flicker. Val was waxy cold.

"I don't think CPR is going to do him any good," Jack said.

Angelina looked up at him and brushed a strand of black hair back from her face.

"You're right. I just thought it would be good to try."

Both Jack and Angelina stood up and waited for Sally to finish her call. It didn't take her long.

When she hung up, Jack asked, "What's going on?"

Sally said, "Val's dead, I think. I'm going to call Eric Desmond. Would you mind dismissing Val's class?"

"He's dead, all right," Jack said, admiring Sally's calm demeanor. He didn't feel at all calm himself, and he wished he could be as composed as she seemed to be. "Where's the class being held?"

Sally told him, and he went to the classroom. He informed the students who were still there that Mr. Hurley was ill, which was true enough, depending on how you looked at it, and said that they should check the syllabus for their next assignment.

"We don't have a syllabus," said a young woman in the second row. A gold stud stood out from her right nostril like a large pimple.

"Well, then," Jack said, "just consider that today's assignment will be carried over until next time."

74

"Will Mr. Hurley be back?" someone asked from the back of the room.

"I don't think so," Jack said, thinking about Val's bloody head and not wanting to lie. "But you can be sure that someone will be here to teach you."

"I hope so," the girl with the nose stud said. "I paid good money for this class."

No one paid her much attention. Everyone else was too busy gathering up notebooks and getting out of there.

When everyone had left, Jack went back down to Val's office. Sally, or someone, had closed the door. Jack didn't know whether to go in, knock, or just leave. He'd about decided to leave when the door of the gallery opened and Eric Desmond sauntered in.

Desmond was head of the Hughes Community College Security Office, or, in other words, the chief of the campus police. He didn't look like a cop, however—or at least not like what Jack thought cops should look like. First-time visitors to the campus often thought Desmond must be the president until they heard his title. He dressed almost as well as Harold Fieldstone, though a good bit flashier, and he was a fanatical fitness buff. Desmond could be seen on the college track every day at noon, running anywhere from five to eight miles. He also worked out in the weight room for at least an hour a day, watched his diet, and took handfuls of vitamins with every meal. He was ruggedly handsome, and although he was nearly sixty years old, he didn't look much over forty.

"Where's the body?" he asked Jack.

Desmond's voice was as calm as Sally's had been, maybe calmer. Jack decided that other people were simply better at dealing with emergencies than he was.

Jack pointed a thumb at the closed door. "In the office. Dr. Good's in there. Ms. Sanchez is with her. She tried CPR, but it didn't do any good."

"Too bad," Desmond said. "Hurley was an okay guy." He paused for a moment as if out of respect, and then continued. "I don't think you should hang around here, Neville. This is police business now."

"I might be able to help," Jack said, immediately wondering why he'd opened his mouth. He couldn't think of a thing he could do.

Desmond shrugged. "All right, you can stay, but keep out of the office. In fact, if you want to be useful, why don't you go to the parking lot and keep a lookout for the locals? Dr. Good says she gave them a call, and they should be here in a few minutes. There'll be an ambulance, too."

Jack nodded and left the gallery. The parking lot was on the other side of the building, and he walked around there, stood in the sunshine, and waited.

It wasn't long before the ambulance arrived. Jack sent the EMTs up to Val's office and continued to wait. Within minutes, a big white Chevrolet came roaring into the lot and squealed to a stop in a "No Parking" zone not far from where he stood. The words *Hughes Police Department* were painted on the side of the car in red and blue script.

Two officers got out of the car, one in uniform and one in plain clothes. The uniformed cop glanced over at the ambulance and then asked where the crime scene was. Jack volunteered to take the two men there, and they trooped up the stairs behind him, neither of them saying a word. Jack figured they didn't have anything to say to civilians.

The door to Val's office was open again when they got there, and the two men shouldered Jack aside to greet Desmond. Jack got another glimpse of Val's body, this time with the EMTs looking at it and saying something to Desmond. Probably telling him that there wasn't anything they could do for Val.

Jack waved a hand to get Sally's attention. He'd seen

enough television crime shows to know that she was going to be there a long time while the cops questioned her.

"Want me to take care of any classes for you?" he asked.

She shook her head. Maybe she didn't have classes until the afternoon, or maybe she didn't watch TV crime shows. Jack smiled at her, and then he started to leave.

"Where do you think you're going, fella?" the uniformed cop asked. He was a short, blocky man with thick black hair on the backs of his hands.

"Back to my office," Jack said.

"Nobody leaves the premises," the officer said. "Right, Chief Desmond?"

"It's all right for him to go," Desmond said. "He didn't find the body. He just wandered onto the scene."

The officer didn't look happy to hear that news, but he told Jack that he could leave.

Jack left the building again and headed back to his office. For the first time, he began to feel the full impact of what had happened. Val Hurley was dead. And he wasn't just dead; he'd most likely been murdered.

For a moment or so, Jack thought he might be sick to his stomach. He'd seen dead bodies before, sure, but they'd always been in funeral homes, safely stowed in caskets. And they'd all died of what people liked to call "natural causes." They hadn't been lying on their office floors, and they certainly hadn't been conked in the head with little statues of *Winged Victory*.

Or maybe Val hadn't been conked in the head at all. On some of the crime shows that Jack had seen, there were very clever criminals who planted false clues to throw off the police. Maybe that's what the statue was—a false clue.

Somehow, though, Jack didn't think so. He thought it was a real clue, and he was sure that Desmond and the two local cops would think so, too.

Which meant that there was a killer in Hughes, Texas, maybe even on the college campus right that minute. That thought made Jack's stomach churn a little faster.

As Jack walked back to his office, James Naylor passed him going the other way. Naylor's head was down, and the dean looked distracted. Jack didn't blame him. Fieldstone had probably called him with the bad news.

Jack turned to see where Naylor went. Sure enough, the dean was headed straight for the president's office. Naylor was slick, smart, and had a way with words, as Jack well knew, but no amount of fast talking was going to smooth over the murder of a faculty member.

For the first time, Jack wondered who'd done it. A couple of suspects immediately popped into his head, and he wondered who else knew what he did about certain members of the faculty.

He also wondered whether he should tell the police. He decided that he would if they asked. Otherwise, he was going to keep his mouth shut.

If he didn't, someone might start to think that *he* had a motive to kill Val Hurley, which was, of course, totally ridiculous. Unfortunately, the police might not see it that way, since he had practically the same motive as a couple of other people had.

Better not to think about it. Better to think about his Buddy Holly article, which was almost finished. He could go back to his office and polish it up a bit more, and then grade a few papers before his World Literature class, which would be discussing *Medea*.

For some reason, thinking of *Medea* brought him right back to Val Hurley. He knew he was making some kind of unconscious connection between Val's death and the tragedy of Jason, not that Val was any mythological hero. But Medea had killed Jason's sons out of revenge. What was that line in the play? Something about how a woman wronged in love was capable of anything.

Jack shook his head as if trying to shake the thought out of it, but it was no use. He couldn't quit thinking about Medea and her revenge. It was going to be a long day.

13

Sally Good popped the last bite of the Hershey bar into her mouth, leaned back in her chair, and savored the sweet taste of the chocolate and the crunch of the nut. She'd had a hard day, as well as a long one, and if anyone at Hughes College deserved a Hershey bar with almonds, she did.

After a few seconds of savoring the chocolate, Sally took a few swallows of water from the plastic bottle on her desk. It wasn't really designer water, though it had a designer label. She'd drunk the original water, which had tasted just fine, but since then she'd refilled the bottle several times from her home water faucet. That water was a lot cheaper, and Sally didn't notice much difference in the taste.

She set the bottle back on the desk and allowed herself to think about what had happened to Val Hurley. Poor Val. The police had concluded that he'd been killed by the little statue of *Winged Victory* that she had seen on his desk so many times.

"Crime of opportunity," Eric Desmond had said. "Someone came in, saw the statue, and clobbered him."

The local plainclothesman, whose name was Weems,

hadn't agreed. "Crime of passion, most likely. Someone had to be pretty upset to hit him hard enough to crack his head open."

Weems was tall, thick-waisted, and sure of himself. He spoke as if he investigated murder cases all the time, though Sally knew that there were very few murders in Hughes.

Sally wondered what Val had done to make someone angry enough to kill him. And she wondered who the someone could possibly be. Could there be any connection to the missing picture?

"It's always a possibility," Weems had said when she'd asked him about it during what had seemed to be an endless question-and-answer session.

But it was clear that he didn't really think so. It was also clear that he wasn't going to take any suggestions from some woman English teacher who didn't know the first thing about police investigative procedures.

So Sally had answered all his questions as best she could, though she wasn't of much help. It wasn't her fault that she didn't know about Val's enemies—or whether he even had any. She'd been his division chair, not his best friend.

Of course, there were always the Thompsons. Weems's eyes lit up like halogen lamps when Sally mentioned the Thompsons. Here was something he could believe in.

Sally wasn't sure how much of the story she should tell, but Fieldstone wasn't around to advise her about the best interests of the college, and it was a murder case, after all. So she told the whole thing, only slightly edited for the protection of the school.

"I'll bet the husband was really pissed when he found out his wife was posing nude," Weems said.

He was so pleased with the possibility of real suspects that he was practically rubbing his hands together. To Sally, he looked like a man who badly wanted to make an arrest and get things all tidied up before the news of the murder even got out. Fieldstone and Naylor would love him.

"I have no idea what the husband thought," Sally said. "I tried to call him last night, but I wasn't able to get in touch with him."

"He's skipped?" Weems said, looking more pleased than ever. "That's very interesting. Excuse me for a minute."

The uniformed policeman, assisted by Desmond, had been going over the crime scene, taking pictures and measurements, maybe even dusting for fingerprints. Sally wasn't sure about that part, since Weems had asked her if there was somewhere they could go for a chat. They had been sitting in an empty classroom, which Weems now left.

After a few seconds, he was back. "I called in to have a check run on the Thompson guy," he said.

Sally wondered what they would find out. Probably nothing.

Weems continued to question Sally for a while, but she finally convinced him that she'd told all she knew. He gave in and said that she could go but that she should "keep herself available" for further questioning.

Sally said that she would be right there on campus or at home and left the gallery. What she wanted right then more than anything was a Hershey bar. Or two.

She'd settled for one. After she licked the last traces of the chocolate from her fingers and wiped them on a tissue from her purse, she tossed the tissue in the trash can.

It was time to go home. She'd been hiding behind the closed door of her office for most of the afternoon, and she hadn't answered any of her calls, not even the one from Fieldstone. The calls had been picked up by her answering machine, and she could return them tomorrow.

If she felt like it. Only the one from Fieldstone really mattered. The others were from faculty members who'd heard about Val and wanted to find out what Sally knew.

She wasn't sure how much she knew, but she was sure that she wasn't going to tell anything. One thing she'd learned in her tenure as a quasi-administrator was that the less she said about anything the least bit controversial, the better off she'd be in the long run.

She looked at her desk and thought for a millisecond about trying to straighten it. No, she wasn't that desperate for a distraction.

She told herself not to worry about Val's death. The police were on the job, and they'd soon figure out who'd killed him. She knew that Desmond had taken the guest register from its white column, and she supposed it was always possible that the killer had been stupid enough to sign in.

She thought she could figure out Desmond's reasoning. To him, it was a crime of opportunity. Someone had come into the gallery, signed the book, and later happened to see Val in his office. The murder had happened and the killer had left, forgetting in his haste to rip out the register page with his name on it.

Sally wondered why she was thinking of the killer as "he." Val had had plenty of relationships with women. Vera Vaughn for one. He could just as easily have been killed by one of them as by a man. While Vera might object to being considered a suspect, she would have to admit that Sally should give her an equal opportunity.

It was too bad that the gallery didn't have a security camera. Sally had suggested that one be installed a year or so earlier, but no one had thought that student paintings were worth the expense.

Desmond had been the leader of the opposition, in fact, arguing that to cover the gallery properly, at least three cameras would have to be installed.

"And who'd want to steal any of that stuff?" he'd said. "Amateur art is what it is. Some of that stuff looks like they just threw the paint on the canvas and smeared it around with their fingers, like kids in kindergarten."

Fieldstone and Naylor had agreed with him, so there had been no cameras installed. Now, however, the camera might have proved its usefulness, and Sally would have bet a month's salary that one or two or three would soon be put in place. The school was great at closing barn doors after the horses had already disappeared.

Sally wondered again about the missing painting. There was a student painting gone now, and it certainly wasn't any masterpiece. Why had someone taken it? She might not even have noticed that it was gone if there hadn't already been a problem about it, but now she felt that it was a part of the solution to the crime.

Find out who took the painting, she thought, and you'd have Val's killer.

Not that she had any intention of trying to find out who had taken the painting. All she wanted to do was go home, give Lola a kitty treat, and take a nice warm bath.

But of course, she didn't get the chance.

14

Ellen Baldree was standing just outside Sally's office door, her hand raised to knock. Both she and Sally were startled, and Ellen dropped her hand, narrowly avoiding hitting Sally in the face.

Not that she tried too hard to avoid it. Ellen was Sally's one genuine enemy among the Hughes Community College English faculty. She had applied for the division chairmanship before Sally's hiring, and she was still thoroughly resentful that an outsider like Sally had been chosen instead of herself.

Nothing that Sally did met with Ellen's approval, and Ellen often worked in subtle ways to undermine any changes that Sally tried to make. Sally had once overheard Ellen saying, "I've outlasted two other department chairs, and I'll outlast this one." Sally had been tempted to say, "We'll see about that, dear," but she had refrained. She didn't want to be accused of eavesdropping.

"Oh, you're still here," Ellen said, smiling, as if to imply that Sally left the campus early every afternoon. "I was wondering if I could talk to you about a little matter that's come up."

"Certainly," Sally said, resisting the urge to heave a heavy sigh. "Come in and have a seat."

Sally sat at her desk, and Ellen sat in the chair beside it. She was a short woman of about fifty-five with dark eyes and short hair that was dyed an amazing shade of black, so black that it almost seemed to absorb the light around it.

"I suppose you've heard about Val Hurley," Ellen said.

Sally nodded. "Yes. I've heard."

Ellen turned slightly sideways and leaned on Sally's desk, or rather on one of the piles of paper that lined the edge.

"You know, of course, that he was playing around with a student," Ellen said.

Sally frowned, not trying to hide her disapproval of the direct statement.

"I don't believe that's been proven."

"Ha," Ellen said, showing what she thought of the necessity of proof. "You're his division chair, and as you must know, you're responsible for his behavior. So naturally, I thought you'd be informed about what was going on."

Sally took a deep breath. "I'm not responsible for Val's behavior any more than I am for yours."

Ellen drew back. "And what is that supposed to mean?"

"It means that I'm not anyone's keeper. What people do on their own time is no concern of mine."

"We're talking about a student here. And an incident that occurred on school property. In any lawsuit, you could be held liable."

Sally didn't want to get into a discussion of the law with Ellen Baldree, who probably knew even less about it than Sally did, if that was possible. But she was beginning to get an idea of why Ellen had come by, so she decided to cut through the nonsense.

"Are you hoping that I'll be fired because of Val's murder?" she asked.

Ellen pretended to be shocked. "Of course not! How can you say such a thing? I was simply concerned about you. A person in your position can't be too careful." She stood up huffily. "I can see that you don't want my sympathy or advice, however, so I'll be going."

She was almost out the door when Sally remembered that one of the only people who seemed able to tolerate Ellen for more than a few minutes was Vera Vaughn.

"Does Vera know about Val?" she asked.

Ellen turned back. "Yes. I talked to her a little while ago. She's naturally very upset."

Sally wasn't sure how true this was. She had never quite been able to figure out what Vera had seen in Val. But then Vera had dated nearly every unmarried man on the faculty, and some of the married ones, at one time or another. None of her romances seemed to last long. Maybe it had something to do with her philosophy.

Sally thought of something else. "Didn't you go out with Val at one time?"

Ellen started, recovered, and said, "No. He was—"

—much too young for you, Sally thought uncharitably.

"—not my type," Ellen finished.

"Well, then, thanks for coming by," Sally said. "I appreciate your support."

Ellen, who either didn't understand irony or preferred to ignore it, didn't reply. She turned and left the office.

Sally listened to Ellen's heels clicking down the hallway and wondered why Ellen had lied about her relationship with Val. Hughes was a small college, and things got around quickly. One story that had gone around a year or so ago was that Val Hurley was going out with Ellen, a story that caused a little talk mainly because Val was at least fifteen years younger than Ellen.

Vera Vaughn had been the first one to point out that if the ages had been reversed, that if Val had been the one fifteen years older, no one would have said a word.

Val had broken up with Ellen not long after that, but it had been a while before he'd begun dating Vera.

Sally shook her head. All that was old news, and it had nothing to do with Val's death. What she had to do now was find someone to teach Val's classes. She couldn't leave until that was done.

She looked through the drawers of her filing cabinet, hoping to run across the telephone numbers of some of the people who had applied for part-time jobs. Because her filing system consisted of stacking things in the drawer, the search took a while. But at least the applications were there, buried under purchase orders, course plans, grade-change applications, and the like. In less than an hour, Sally had people lined up to come in and take over where Val had left off.

Wherever that was. She knew that Val didn't follow a course outline. But that would matter only in a class like Art Appreciation or Art History. In Painting or Watercolor, it was a different story.

Sally hoped that the students could adjust to the new instructors, and then realized that young people seemed to be more flexible than their elders gave them credit for. There was no need for her to worry about them. It was the faculty that would have a hard time adjusting to the fact that one of their number had died violently at the hand of another.

Sally looked around the office. There wasn't really much else that she could do there, unless she wanted to clean the place up, which she had no intention of doing. So she gathered up a few papers, fooling herself into believing that she'd grade them at home, and left.

15

Val's murder was the talk of the faculty lounge the next morning, along with the fact that the faculty lottery pool had once again failed to win the big jackpot. The twenty-two people in the pool had each pitched in five dollars, allowing them to buy a hundred and ten tickets. Out of that number, they'd had three matches of three numbers each, for a grand total of nine dollars in winnings.

Sally was reminded of the old joke about how to make a small fortune: begin with a large one. At the same time, she knew she'd kick in her five bucks for the next pool, not because she thought they might win but because she knew she wouldn't be able to live with herself if everyone else won and retired without her.

But the pool results were of only minor interest today. What everyone wanted to talk about was Val Hurley, and of course it was Troy Beauchamp who had all the scoop. Whether Troy's stories had any basis in reality was entirely beside the point. He was able to relate them with such gusto and authority that he convinced everyone that they were the absolute gospel.

His first theory was that Vera Vaughn was the killer.

"Vera wouldn't kill anybody with a statue," Jeff Hayes said. "She has other methods."

Hayes was young, not quite thirty, and ambitious. He sucked up to the administrators at every opportunity, even having gone so far as to compliment Fieldstone on his suspenders on one occasion. Hayes didn't mind letting everyone know that he had his eye on Naylor's job and that his application would be on top of the stack when the dean retired.

"What methods would those be?" Gary Borden asked.

Borden was wearing a wide green tie with mushrooms on it. Sally thought they were probably supposed to be some kind of sixties symbol. Psychedelic mushrooms, maybe.

"You mean you don't know?" Hayes asked.

"I'm a married man," Borden said. "So I wouldn't have any idea."

Hayes grinned. "Married or not, that never made much difference to Vera."

"Come on, guys," Jack Neville said. "We wouldn't be talking this way if Vera were here."

"Sure we would," Hayes said. "But we're getting off the subject. Why would Vera have killed Val, Troy?"

Beauchamp was ready with the answer. "Because he dropped her for someone else." He paused. "A student."

"Maybe Vera killed him because he was guilty of sexual harassment," Wylie Reese said.

Reese was the chair of Math and Sciences. He was known to his faculty as "Mr. Meetings" because he loved to have his department meet to discuss everything that came up, no matter how trivial. He had even been known to call meetings on Friday afternoons, thus ending any chance he might have had of being voted most popular chair on campus.

"That's a good point, knowing Vera," Beauchamp said. "But a person with a better right to that motive would be Ms. Thompson's husband. He might have tried to talk to Val and lost his temper and killed him with the first thing that came to hand."

Sally wondered if the police had been able to find the Thompsons. So she asked Troy.

"I don't know," he admitted. "But they're the most likely suspects. Tammi may have killed Val herself because of what he did. Or maybe she was romantically involved with him and didn't want her husband to find out. The only way out was to accuse Val of harassment and then kill him to make sure he couldn't defend himself against the accusation."

"Are you saying she led him on?" Gary Borden asked, trying to lead Troy on.

"Absolutely not," Beauchamp said, smiling to show that he'd recognized the trap. "I'd never suggest such a thing."

"That's good," Borden said. "Because if you did, and if Vera heard about it, she might kill you."

No one laughed.

"What about A. B. D. Johnson?" Samuel Winston asked, staring owlishly around. "He was really upset about Val's chair. He even came by my office to complain."

"He complained to a lot of people," Troy said. "Even me. But do you think he'd kill someone over a chair?"

"Why not?" Winston said. "A. B. D.'s always wound a little tight. Maybe he lost his temper, grabbed that statue, and smashed in Val's head with it."

Everyone thought about that for a minute. People knew that Johnson was high-strung, and more than one person had remarked that he was likely to snap one day.

Sally didn't think so, however. "What about the missing painting?" she asked.

"Painting?" Troy Beauchamp said. "What painting?"

Sally told them about the painting of the goat.

"Oh, the one Roy Don Talon complained about," Beauchamp said.

Once again, Sally was amazed at Troy's knowledge of everything that went on at the college. She would have bet that no one in the meeting with Talon would have discussed it, but obviously someone had.

"That's the painting, all right," she said. "It's missing. Someone must have taken it from the gallery."

Troy had to tell the others the story of the painting. When he was finished, he said, "So that gives us another potential killer: Roy Don Talon. He got into an argument with Val about the picture and killed him. Then he took the picture down so none of HCC's innocent students would be corrupted by the image of the beast."

"We were going to have a jury look at the picture and decide whether it was a Satanic symbol," Sally said. "Mr. Talon knew that."

Beauchamp wasn't dissuaded. "He probably figured out that the jury was just a trick to keep the picture up and decided to get rid of it himself. But really, none of our speculations is needed. Chief Desmond will have come up with the killer's name by now."

"And how will he have done that?" Samuel Winston asked.

"Clever police work," Troy told him. "If the police have an approximate time of death, all Desmond has to do is check the guest register. The person who was in the gallery nearest that time will be the killer."

"Right," Jeff Hayes said. "The killer signed his name and put down the time of his visit just to make it easy for the campus flatfeet." He glanced up at the electric clock on the wall. "I wish I had time to continue this fascinating discussion, but I don't. I happen to have an eight o'clock class."

So did nearly everyone else in the lounge, and they all began to file out, leaving only Sally and Jack Neville behind.

"What do you think the police have really found out?" Jack asked her.

"Nothing, probably. I know they were interested in questioning the Thompsons, but that's all."

"You don't think they're looking at jealousy as a motive, do you?"

There was a thin line of sweat on Jack's upper lip, and Sally wondered why he looked so guilty all of a sudden.

"Why do you ask?" she said. "Are you worried?"

Jack chuckled weakly. "No, no, of course not. I was just wondering about what the police might think. I dated Vera for a while, you know."

"If they suspect everyone who dated Vera, they'll have a long list," Sally said. "I think you're in the clear."

"I hope so," Jack said. "Well, I have an eight o'clock, too. I don't want to be too late."

As he headed for the door, Sally watched him go. And she wondered again why he looked so guilty.

16

As she was walking back to her office, Sally met Jorge Rodriguez. He was wearing a black suit with gray pinstripes that did nothing to minimize his bulk. He looked able to leap tall buildings in a single bound.

"I hear that we won't have to worry about that painting any more," he said. "It's gone, isn't it?"

"Yes," Sally said. "But we have a lot more to worry about now."

Jorge nodded slightly. "True, but not for long. Everyone knows that Desmond will crack the case today."

"You have a lot more faith in him than I do," Sally said.

Jorge smiled. "I've had more experience with the police than you have, as well. I know how those guys work."

Sally blushed and hoped she hadn't embarrassed him. She hadn't meant to imply anything.

"Can you come in my office and talk for a minute?" she asked.

"Sure," Jorge said.

Sally was glad he didn't ask why, though the reason was

simple enough. It wasn't that she wanted to get him alone, and she hoped he didn't think that. It was just that she didn't like talking in the hallway. There were poorly insulated classrooms along both sides, and their conversation might be disturbing the students even if they couldn't quite make out the words.

When they were inside her office, Sally closed the door and moved a stack of papers from the chair by her desk.

"Have a seat," she told Jorge, going to her own chair. Then she asked, "How close can the medical examiner come to determining a time of death?"

"You think I'm an expert?" Jorge asked.

Sally blushed again. "I didn't mean to suggest anything. I just thought you might know."

Jorge smiled, showing those amazingly white teeth. "I'm not offended. Anyway, the M.E. can come pretty close to a time of death, but it's still going to be just an estimate. And it'll be a while before we get any information at all. Every county around here sends bodies to Houston for autopsy, and sometimes it's weeks before the results are sent back. Why do you ask?"

"I was just wondering when Val might have been killed. If it was yesterday morning, that means students might have been in the building when he died."

Jorge knew immediately that she wasn't worried about the students having overheard anything.

"And you think they might have seen someone coming out of his office," he said.

"That's right. And it could be that they saw someone take the painting. I wonder if Chief Desmond is going to question any of them."

"He's going to leave everything to the locals," Jorge said. "Unless of course they ask for his help. That's the best thing to do, believe me. Desmond's not a bad cop, but he doesn't

want to get mixed up in a murder. He's too smart for that."
Jorge gave Sally a sharp look. "I hope you aren't thinking
about doing any amateur investigating."

"Oh, no," Sally said. "Not me. I don't know the first thing
about it. I'm not going to get involved."

But as she said she wasn't, she realized that she was considering it. She didn't think Weems was going about things
the right way at all. He wasn't interested in the missing painting. He didn't even ask for Val's class roll so he could talk to
the students. All he could think about was the Thompsons.

She said as much to Jorge, who frowned. "The cops always
go for a quick arrest. It makes them look bad if they don't
come up with someone fairly quickly, or at least they think
it does. So if there's a handy suspect with a good motive
and no alibi, they'll make an arrest. You can't really blame
them."

Sally wondered if he was speaking from experience. She
imagined Jorge as the Wronged Innocent, the man sent to
prison to suffer for the crimes of another because the police
had rushed to justice. She thought of him in his prison whites,
his muscles bulging as he broke rocks in the hot sun with a
sledgehammer, all the while enduring a punishment intended
for someone else.

She blinked the vision away and said, "You mean the police would arrest someone they knew was innocent?"

"No. They wouldn't do that. Not if they were certain. But
they want to close the case, and if there's a likely looking
suspect, then he'd better watch out. And look at it this way:
about nine-tenths of the time, they get the right person."

Sally didn't like the whole idea of it. "What about the other
one-tenth? What about those people?"

"They're the ones who'd better get themselves really good
lawyers."

It was on the tip of Sally's tongue to ask Jorge what kind

of lawyer he'd had, but she thought better of it. She imagined a public defender, barely out of his teens, who'd passed the bar exam a month before the trial, who was still heavily into Clearasil use and shaving only every third day or so, and whose client was doomed to spend time in prison for a crime he never committed.

"If I were you," Jorge said, "I'd forget about the whole thing. Just teach your classes and let the police do their job. That's what we pay them for."

"That's probably a very good idea," Sally said.

She might have said more, but the phone rang just then, and Jorge excused himself.

Watching his broad shoulders pass through her doorway, Sally picked up the phone.

"This is Dr. Good," she said. "How may I help you?"

"Dr. Good?"

People always said that, though Sally invariably answered the phone by giving her name. She could never quite understand why no one ever believed her when she told them who she was. Or maybe they just weren't listening.

"Yes," she said. "This is Dr. Good."

"Oh. Well, this is Amy Willis. In the business office?"

Sally had dealt with Amy Willis before. She was responsible for the payroll, and she kept up with all the departmental budget accounts. Possibly because of her fiscal responsibilities, or possibly because it was simply her nature, Amy had more tics than anyone Sally had ever met.

She never seemed to sit still. She tapped her fingers and patted her feet. When she talked, her hands were in constant motion. Even her hair seemed at times to be twitching around on her head.

"I need to talk to you about a confidential matter," Amy said. "Can you come over to the Business Office?"

Sally looked at her watch. She really needed to grade some of those papers.

"Can it wait until this afternoon?"

"Not really," Amy said. "It's about Mr. Hurley."

"I'll be right over," Sally told her.

17

Sally left her office, turned the corner, and nearly collided with A. B. D. Johnson. He wasn't in any of his usual stages of dudgeon, which was surprising in itself. Even more surprisingly, he looked distraught.

"I have to talk to you," he said, his jowls quivering.

"I'm on my way to a meeting," Sally told him, which, while it wasn't exactly the truth, was close enough and might discourage him.

"This is important," A. B. D. said, as if to imply that college meetings weren't, a fact that Sally couldn't really argue with. "I'll only take a minute."

There was an undertone of desperation in his voice, and Sally gave in.

"I can give you a minute, but that's it."

She turned back to her office, and A. B. D. followed like a despondent basset hound. As soon as they were inside, A. B. D. closed the door behind him.

"I didn't kill Val Hurley," he said, looking uncannily like Richard Nixon proclaiming that he wasn't a crook. If he'd been on trial, the jury would have voted him guilty on all counts, no matter what the counts might have been.

"No one said you killed anyone," Sally assured him, but A. B. D. merely turned a dangerous shade of red, and his eyes widened alarmingly.

"What's the matter?" Sally asked. "Could I get you a drink of water?"

"Don't treat me like a student!" A. B. D. said. "I've used that 'drink of water' bit, myself. You're just trying to calm me down and brush me off!"

"No, I'm not," Sally said, all the while thinking, *Yes, I am.*

"Well, it won't work," A. B. D. said. "You can't get rid of me that easily. I'm probably going to be arrested soon, and it's all Fieldstone's fault."

"Fieldstone?"

"Can't you see that this is the perfect opportunity for him to get rid of me? I know he's had his eye on me for years, just waiting for me to slip up. He thinks I'm a troublemaker, and now he's going to turn me in!"

"But you haven't done anything," Sally said.

A. B. D. suddenly turned shrewd. "How do you know that?"

"Because I'm sure you wouldn't hurt anyone." Sally wasn't sure at all, but it seemed like the right thing to say. "Besides, what had Val ever done to you?"

"He got that new chair, that's what he did. You know that. Why are you denying it?"

"I'm not denying it. I didn't even think of it," Sally lied.

"Of course you thought of it." A. B. D. looked around furtively, as if expecting to discover half the faculty hiding behind the bookshelves and under the desk as they listened in on him. "Everyone's talking about it, and they don't even know about the memo yet."

"Memo? What memo?"

"The memo I wrote to Fieldstone." A. B. D. reached into his shirt pocket and pulled out a folded paper. "Fortunately, I keep copies of everything. That's a lesson I learned a long time ago."

He thrust the memo toward Sally and waved it in her face. She took it from him as much out of self-defense as out of any desire to see what it said.

"Go ahead," A. B. D. said. "Read it."

Sally unfolded the paper and looked at it. It was a standard Hughes Community College memorandum form, and it was directed to Harold Fieldstone.

Sally had a sinking feeling in the pit of her stomach that wasn't due to hypoglycemia. All the same, she wished she had a Hershey bar.

"You didn't say anything . . . incriminating, did you?"

"Just read it," A. B. D. said.

Sally read it. The body of the memo began with a series of complaints about the school's lack of fiscal responsibility over the past few years, shifted to a snide remark about the lack of faculty pay raises, and then brought up the matter of Val Hurley's chair.

The most unfortunate sentence of all was this: "People who have no more compunction than to spend exorbitant amounts of precious college funds on a piece of expensive furniture should be dealt with forthrightly and terminated immediately."

"Oh, my," Sally said.

A. B. D. nodded sadly. "You can see the problem. Obviously I didn't mean *terminated* in the sense of *killed*. I would never suggest something like that. But this is Fieldstone's big chance to get rid of the loyal opposition. He'll have me arrested today. I'm sure of it."

Sally's first inclination was to ask, "So what am I supposed to do?"

Her second inclination was to say, "Think of all the free time you'll have to work on your dissertation while you're in prison."

But either of those things would have been just as foolish as what A. B. D. had written in his memo to Fieldstone, so she didn't say them.

She said, "I'm sure you won't be arrested. I'll talk to Dr. Fieldstone and explain things to him. He's probably been very busy today, and he might not even have had time to read your memo."

"You can't be sure of that! I've taught in the prisons! What if I'm thrown in with some of the people who failed my classes? I wouldn't last a day! Someone would slip a shiv in me before they got the cell door locked!"

A. B. D. was getting worked up, and Sally was getting worried. With his shuddering jowls and his red face, he looked as if he might be capable of just about anything, even murder. Sally began to wonder if maybe he were in need of professional help.

"Don't be ridiculous," she said firmly. "You're in no danger of going to prison. Even if Dr. Fieldstone were to call the police, they wouldn't arrest you on evidence as flimsy as an ambiguous memo. They're too careful for that. After all, they have community relations to think about, and false arrests don't do much to foster a sense of trust. You take everything much too seriously."

A. B. D. was jolted upright. "Too seriously! You don't think being accused of murder is serious?"

"No one's accused you of anything. I think you should take a day or so off from your classes. You could have a talk with Gary Borden. He might know someone who could help you feel better about things."

A. B. D. sank back into his chair and put his hand over his eyes.

"You think I'm crazy, don't you?" he said. Then he leaned forward. "I know you do. Why don't you just come right out and say it?"

"Because it isn't true. You're just . . . overwrought. Just try to think it through. You didn't really say anything to make anyone suspicious. You're making too much out of this. There's nothing for you to be worried about."

"Oh yes, there is. You don't know Fieldstone. He's out to get me."

"I'm supposed to be meeting with him right now," Sally lied, hoping that A. B. D. would remember that he'd promised to keep her only a minute. "I'll tell him that the memo means nothing. That he can just disregard it."

A. B. D. looked hopeful. "Do you think he'll listen to you?"

"I'm sure of it," Sally said, although she knew that Fieldstone never listened to anyone unless he agreed with them.

"Maybe I should go over to his office with you," A. B. D. said. "I could explain about the memo and tell him what I really meant by *terminated*."

"I don't think that would be a good idea," Sally said.

She knew that it wouldn't have been a good idea even if she really did have a meeting with Fieldstone. In fact, it would have been an even worse idea in that case. As it was, she didn't want A. B. D. to find out that she was lying. That wouldn't have done at all.

"Well, all right." A. B. D. was deflated. "I suppose I'll have to trust you."

He didn't look to Sally as if he'd ever trusted anyone, which was probably part of his problem. Except in this case, he was absolutely right not to trust her, since she probably wouldn't see Fieldstone that day at all.

"You don't have a thing to worry about," she assured him. "I'll take care of it."

She stood up. A. B. D. didn't move.

"I have to go now," she said.

"All right." A. B. D. stood up and opened the office door. "Let me know what he says, will you?"

"Of course," Sally said, stepping past him and into the hall.

But I'll have to see him first, she thought.

18

Amy Willis seemed even more nervous than usual. She tapped her short red nails on the top of her desk. She crossed her legs. She uncrossed her legs. She stuck a pencil into her hair, and then took it out and drummed an obscure, jerky beat on the desk.

"I really don't know how to begin," she said as she continued to drum.

"Just tell me why you called," Sally suggested.

They were sitting in Amy's office, which was smaller than Sally's and even less private. While its door didn't open onto a hallway as Sally's did, it did open into a large outer office that was ringed by other offices, all with open doorways. Sally imagined that listening ears were everywhere.

Maybe I've been hanging around A. B. D. Johnson too much, she thought.

"Why don't we close the door?" Sally said.

"That's a good idea," Amy said, getting up.

When the door was closed, she sat back down and started cracking her knuckles.

"You were going to tell me something about Val," Sally said.

Amy sighed. "I don't know where to begin."

Sally was losing her patience. First A. B. D. Johnson and now Amy. It was too much.

"You called me," she pointed out. "If you don't want to tell me anything, I'll just go."

Amy stopped cracking her knuckles and picked up the pencil again. She tapped out a few tentative clicks, then stopped.

"It's not that I don't want to tell you. It's just that nothing like this has ever happened before."

Sally saw her opening. "Like what?"

"Like someone stealing money from the school. I didn't even think it was possible. We have a very efficient system here, with lots of checks and balances. It shouldn't have slipped by."

"What slipped by?"

The tapping increased in intensity. Sally resisted a powerful urge to reach across and grab the pencil out of Amy's hand, and then snap it in two and toss it in the trash can.

As if she sensed Sally's thoughts, Amy put the pencil down and crossed her legs. Her right foot began to jiggle rapidly, but at least it was soundless.

"Mr. Hurley tricked us, is what he did," Amy said.

Sally noted the use of the plural. Consciously or unconsciously, Amy was already beginning to spread the blame around.

"He tricked you?" Sally said.

"That's right. He tricked us. Otherwise, we'd never have let it happen. Surely Dr. Fieldstone will understand. Won't he?"

It was clear from Amy's tone that she didn't really think Fieldstone would understand at all. Sally wondered if everyone on campus except her believed that Fieldstone had received his graduate degree from the Inquisition with Torquemada as his dissertation director.

"Dr. Fieldstone is a very understanding man," Sally said. "I'm sure he won't blame you."

"I hope so. It's not so very much money, after all, when you think about it. Not when you compare it to the college's yearly budget, anyway."

"How much money is it?"

"Five thousand dollars," Amy said.

"Good grief," Sally said.

Amy stiffened and her foot stopped jiggling. "Well, he *tricked* us. It wasn't our fault."

"Tell me about it," Sally said, hoping that maybe this time Amy would actually get to the point.

"Well, you know how all purchase orders have to be signed by the person requesting the order, the budget manager for the department, the division chair, and the dean?"

Sally said that she was quite familiar with the way purchase orders were handled.

"Sure. You probably sign them all the time. All the division chairs do. Do you ever look at them? I mean, *really* look at them?"

Sally tried not to take offense. She knew that there were no doubt people who routinely signed purchase orders without more than a passing glance to see who was asking for money.

"Of course I look at them," she said. "I never sign anything without reading it."

"Did you ever sign one for five thousand dollars?"

"No," Sally said. "I certainly did not."

Amy slumped in her chair. She picked up the pencil, but she was so deflated that she didn't drum out even a tentative beat.

"I was afraid you were going to say that. I'll bet Dean

111

Naylor and Dr. Fieldstone didn't sign it either."

"Sign what?" Sally asked.

Amy opened her top desk drawer and brought out a piece of paper that Sally recognized at once as a purchase order requisition.

"This," Amy said, handing the form to Sally.

Sally saw that it was indeed a request for five thousand dollars. It had been signed not only by Val Hurley but by Naylor, Fieldstone, and herself.

Except that she hadn't signed it. Someone else had forged her name. The signature looked vaguely like her own, but it wouldn't have fooled an expert, or even someone who'd taken the time to examine it carefully.

"I didn't sign this," she said.

Amy nodded, her face twisted in misery.

"That's not Dean Naylor's signature, either," Sally went on after a few seconds of examination. "And it's not Dr. Fieldstone's."

"You're right," Amy said. "I can see that now."

Sally was thinking that Amy was the one who hadn't looked at the P.O. as carefully as she should have.

"So you're saying that you've already sent the check to pay for the materials that Val requisitioned?"

"That's right," Amy said. "That's what we always do when we get a purchase order."

Sally looked at the form. Val had requested a number of art supplies, including canvas, paints, easels, and chemicals. There was really nothing unusual about the order except the amount.

"I thought he was just ordering everything for the whole year," Amy said. "He could have been, couldn't he?"

Sally supposed it was possible. Then she looked to see the name of the supplier: Thompson's Crafts.

Uh-oh, Sally thought.

"The owner of Thompson's Crafts wouldn't be Tammi Thompson, would it?"

"No," Amy said. "It would be her husband, though. His name's Ralph. I think Tammi might work there, too."

Sally looked at the P.O. "Would a craft shop have all these items in stock?"

"I don't know. We usually buy from an art supply place over in Friendswood."

"Were any of these things ever delivered?"

"Not as far as I know," Amy said. "But the check was issued. I called you because you're Mr. Hurley's division chair. What do you think we should do now?"

Amy's use of "we" was beginning to annoy Sally, especially now that she was being included in it. She gave the form back to Amy.

"I'd suggest that *you* bring this to Mr. Danton's attention," Sally said.

Danton was the head of the Business Office. He'd spent several years in the military, and he liked to think that he ran an efficient, mistake-proof operation. He wasn't going to be happy when he found out what had happened. But that was Amy's problem.

Sally's problem was the Thompsons. And what she was going to tell the police.

19

Sally decided not to tell the police anything, at least not for the time being. That was Danton's responsibility, or Fieldstone's. Danton would almost certainly go to the president before taking any action himself, and Fieldstone could decide whether to inform the police.

Sally told herself this was the best course. She'd always been told to follow the chain of command. And, after all, she didn't know that any crime had been committed or that there was any connection between the purchase order and Val's death.

She had to admit, however, that the P.O. was highly suspicious.

For instance, why would Val have been buying supplies from Ralph Thompson? Thompson had no doubt furnished the college with small items from time to time, but he certainly wasn't one of the usual sources of art supplies.

And why would Val have ordered such a large number of supplies? He could have been buying for the whole year, as Amy had suggested, but if that was true, wouldn't he have been more likely to buy from a wholesaler in order to save the school some money?

Sally didn't know the answers to her own questions, but she thought there was an easy way to find out: she could ask the Thompsons.

That is, she could ask them if she could reach them. They weren't answering their telephone, and they weren't returning calls, so what could she do?

She could go visit them at their business, that's what.

She left the Business Office and went outside, where the class change had sent students walking in all directions. Some of them were hurrying, some were strolling along as if they had at least a week before their next class, and others were sitting on benches having a quick smoke.

Several students called out greetings to her. She smiled and waved, but, being in a hurry, she didn't stop to talk. She was nearing the parking lot when she was stopped by Douglas Young, the head librarian, who came out of the Learning Center as she passed by.

As far as Sally could tell, Douglas was more devoted to his job than anyone she'd ever known. Maybe too devoted. He spent a lot of his time patrolling the library with a screwdriver that he used to pry dried gum from underneath the chairs. While he was patrolling, he would caution everyone to keep quiet. He refused to allow anyone to speak above a whisper, even when there was no one nearby to be disturbed. In fact, he pestered students so much that hardly any of them would go into the library unless forced to do so.

His major crusade, however, was not against gum or noise. It was against anyone with an overdue book. He'd once seriously recommended to the Library Committee that anyone with an overdue book get a little visit from the campus police. The committee had wisely decided not to pursue the suggestion.

Sally herself, though she hadn't been visited by the cops, had once gotten a call from Douglas shortly after eight o'clock on a Saturday morning. He had asked if she knew that she had a book that was three days overdue.

Sally didn't know what she'd told him, since she'd been half asleep. Apparently, it hadn't been pleasant, and she was afraid that she might have suggested what Douglas could do with the book, assuming he ever got it back. He hadn't spoken to her for weeks afterward.

Sally kept hoping he would retire, but that was highly unlikely since he was only about forty. She wondered what he wanted with her. She didn't think she'd checked out any books lately.

"Terrible thing about Val Hurley," he said.

"Yes," Sally said, wondering if he'd stopped her just to commiserate about the loss of a colleague. It didn't seem likely. Douglas wasn't known for his sympathetic feelings for others.

"You're Val's division chair, aren't you?"

"I was," Sally said, correcting the verb tense. "I'm not anymore."

Douglas nodded. "Of course . . . of course. But you were his supervisor while he was working here."

Sally couldn't deny it, though she had begun to develop an uneasy feeling about Douglas's intentions. Lately, whenever anyone brought up the fact that she had been Val's division chair, the conversation almost immediately took a turn for the worse.

"There's something I think you should know," Douglas said. "It concerns another of your faculty members, too."

Sally waited until a group of students had walked past, then said, "Who?"

"Coy Webster."

"Oh," Sally said, wondering what Coy Webster had to do

with anything. "He's not exactly *my* faculty member."

Coy worked for a lot of people. He was a part-time English instructor at Hughes, and he had been teaching two or three courses a semester for Sally ever since she had come there. In fact, he had taught for her predecessor for years before that. He also taught for several of the other community colleges in the area.

Sally didn't envy the man. He carried a different briefcase for each of the schools where he taught, and he was constantly on the road from one school to the next. He probably knew which campus he was on only by looking at the briefcase in his hand.

"What about Coy?" she asked.

"Did you know he's been hanging around the Art and Music Building lately?"

Sally hadn't known, but she was sure that Douglas would know. The Learning Center was located right next door to the Art and Music Building, and it would have been easy for Douglas to see who went in and out, if he was interested.

And he would have been interested. He wasn't quite as nosy as Troy Beauchamp—hardly anyone was—but when Douglas wasn't harassing students, he was standing by one of the Learning Center windows, keeping up with the comings and goings of others on the campus.

"Coy's been in there a lot," Douglas went on. "In fact, I think he's been spending the night in there."

Sally wasn't sure that she'd heard correctly. "What?"

"Spending the night. He's here a lot later than most of the regular faculty."

There was a certain amount of resentment among a certain group of the nonteaching employees, some of whom envied the faculty's ability to set their own hours and usually get away from the campus by four o'clock.

"Why would he spend the night there?" Sally asked.

"I certainly don't know. But he's here early in the morning, too."

"There's no place to sleep in the building," Sally pointed out. "Besides, Coy teaches on a lot of other campuses. He doesn't stay on this one."

"All I know is what I've seen," Douglas said. "I just thought that you should know."

"Thank you," Sally said. "I'll see what I can find out."

"He might have been in there the night Val died," Douglas said.

"I don't think so," Sally said. "But I'll look into it."

"You don't seem too worried."

"I'm not. I'm sure that Coy hasn't been sleeping in the Art and Music Building."

"If you say so. But he's been doing *something* in there."

"We'll see."

"Well," Douglas said with a shrug. "I've done what I could."

He turned and walked back toward the Learning Center. Most of the students were inside the buildings now, waiting for class to get started, and Sally started for the parking lot again.

She was almost to her car when Jack Neville caught up with her.

"I have to talk to you," he said.

20

Jack had been thinking most of the day about Val Hurley. He had even let his mind drift during his American Literature class, and he'd been embarrassed when he found himself talking about Nathaniel Hawthorne's friend "Hurley Melville." A couple of students, the ones who were actually listening to his lecture, had laughed nervously, but Jack had saved himself from making things worse by ignoring his error and going on.

However, he knew that he had to talk to someone about what was bothering him, and the someone he wanted to talk to was Sally Good.

He told himself that he wanted to talk to her because she was his supervisor, but he knew there was more to it than that. He was attracted to Sally, and he wanted to get to know her better.

Getting to know her better wasn't the right thing to do. What could be more fraught with trouble than a romantic relationship with your supervisor?

Nothing, that's what. Jack was well aware of this, and he

told himself that he would keep everything on a strictly professional level. Besides, he was pretty sure that Sally didn't have any romantic interest in him. She didn't date people at Hughes, and if she did, Jack thought she would probably pick Jorge Rodriguez.

Not that he could blame her. Rodriguez was rugged, handsome, and had a romantic outlaw past. Jack was sure that women couldn't resist that part.

What bothered Jack even more than his belief that Sally would choose Rodriguez over him, however, was that Jack had seen Rodriguez sitting with Vera Vaughn in the Seahorse the evening before Val Hurley was murdered.

Assuming that Val had been killed later that night, which Jack thought to be the case, either Jorge and Vera together, or either of them alone, could have easily gone back to the campus and killed Val.

Of course, Val could have died the next morning, shortly before he'd been found, but Jack had discarded that idea since Val wasn't known to be an early riser. He was one of those who always got to campus only a few minutes before his first class, unlike Jack, who liked to get there in time to sit quietly and go over his lesson plans for the day. And, Jack recalled, Val's body had been quite cold.

Jack told himself that there wasn't anything really suspicious about Rodriguez and Vera quietly talking in a back booth in the Seahorse. There was certainly nothing wrong in having a bit of friendly conversation with a colleague.

But Jorge, having served time for murder, wasn't exactly an ordinary colleague. And besides, Jack couldn't help wondering if maybe Vera and Jorge were beginning a romance. Vera never stayed with anyone for very long, something that Jack knew from experience.

In fact, Jack hoped that the police didn't get around to questioning him about Val's death since it was generally well known around campus that he had been pretty upset when Vera had broken up with him.

He hadn't sought her company in the first place. He was much too reserved for that. She had come to his office one afternoon, seated herself in the chair by his desk, crossed her legs, smoothed her leather skirt, and said, "What's your problem, Jack?"

For a minute, he thought she'd discovered his addiction to Minesweeper, but it turned out that wasn't what she'd had in mind at all.

"You haven't said more than two words to me since you started to work here," she said. "What's the matter? Don't you find me attractive?"

Jack hadn't known how to answer. He'd heard that Vera was a sexually liberated woman, but he would never in a million years have expected her to approach him. Maybe he represented a challenge.

At any rate, it hadn't taken Vera long to have her way with him—not that Jack had any complaints about that. He'd been more than willing to be seduced, and he'd enjoyed every minute of it.

Then, when she was through with him, she'd dropped him like a hot horseshoe.

He'd taken it hard, but it wasn't long before several of her other rejects had told him that whatever had happened wasn't his fault.

"That's just Vera," was the common refrain. "She doesn't really like men very much, and she's getting her revenge on us, one at a time."

The realization that he was just one of a large group of rejected lovers didn't make Jack feel any better. In some ways, it made him feel worse, and he'd made some intemperate remarks, which he hadn't meant at all, about what he'd like to do to some of Vera's recent conquests. He hoped the police didn't hear about those comments. If they did, he might find himself called in for questioning. He didn't like the idea of that at all.

Given Vera's track record, Jack had always wondered why Vera hadn't gotten around to Jorge long before now. If there was ever a guy she'd want to get revenge on, he should have been the one, if you believed some of the stories about him. On the other hand, if you believed some of the other stories, maybe he wasn't the kind of man she'd want revenge on at all.

It was too complicated for Jack, which is why he wanted to talk it over with someone, preferably Sally. What if Vera had gone to tell Val that she was through with him and things had turned ugly? She might have beaned him with the statue in the heat of the moment.

Or what if Jorge had been with her? Jorge had already beaned one guy, if you believed the stories. Maybe he had a terrible temper, or maybe things simply got out of control.

So Jack had gone looking for Sally to see what she thought, but she hadn't been in her office, and he hadn't known where else to look.

Then he'd bumped into A. B. D. Johnson and asked him if he'd seen her. A. B. D. told him that Dr. Good was most likely in a meeting with Dr. Fieldstone, so Jack had trekked across campus toward Fieldstone's office in time to see Sally going toward the parking lot.

When he told her that he needed to talk to her, she didn't seem eager to listen.

"I'm really in sort of a hurry," she said. "Is there some problem?"

"I'm not sure," Jack replied. "It's about Val Hurley. Well, it's not exactly about Val, but it might be. It's about someone else, but it could involve Val, if you know what I mean."

"I don't," Sally said.

Jack couldn't blame her. He knew he was babbling. But he couldn't stop.

"I mean, it's something that maybe we shouldn't talk about here in the parking lot," he said. "It could be that it has something to do with Val's death. It probably doesn't, but it might. It's the kind of thing that, well, I'm not even sure I should be talking about it."

"Do you know that you're not making any sense at all?" Sally asked.

Jack's shoulders slumped. "I know. I can't seem to organize my thoughts. If I were writing a freshman essay, I'd have flunked by now."

Sally smiled. "Maybe you should have done some pre-writing." She paused and looked at him. "I'll tell you what. I have to run an errand right now, but maybe you could go along and keep me company. We could talk on the way."

"Sure." Jack tried not to sound overly eager. "Great. That would be fine."

"My car's right over here," Sally said, leading the way to the Acura. "There's not much room, but maybe you can squeeze in."

"I'll manage," Jack said.

When Sally unlocked the door, he folded himself into the front seat. Getting hold of the seat belt and buckling it would have been easier if he'd been a contortionist, though Sally seemed to manage quite easily.

After he'd settled himself, he glanced at the console between them and saw a CD jewel case: Bobby Vee, the "Legendary Masters" series.

"You like Bobby Vee?" he asked, finding it hard to believe that anyone these days even remembered Bobby Vee. Sally had hidden depths.

"Sure," she said. "I think Bobby Vee's great. Play the CD if you want to."

Jack found opening the CD case was almost as tricky as fastening the seat belt, but soon Bobby Vee was singing "Susie Baby."

"Great song," Jack said. "It wasn't a big hit, though."

"What about 'Rubber Ball'?"

"That one was. I like some of the double-tracked numbers, and that's one of the best. Vee's an underrated singer. Hardly anybody plays his hit songs on the radio these days, much less something like 'Stayin' In.' Did you know that one was banned on some stations when it came out?"

Sally said that she didn't, and Jack told her the story. Then he got to the point and told her his suspicions about Vera and Jorge.

21

Sally didn't give Jack's idea much credence.

"You're making too much of nothing," she said. "What did you really see? Two people talking? They were within walking distance of the Art and Music building, but what does that prove? Nothing. So were you. So were Troy Beauchamp and Samuel Winston. You don't think they killed Val, do you?"

Jack was scrunched down in the seat, which was about the only way he *could* sit in the Acura. He looked out the window. They were passing by one of the seventeen (by Jack's count) pizza places in town. If you liked pizza, Hughes was a great place to live.

"When you put it that way, it sounds pretty silly," he said, turning back to look at Sally. "I guess I let my imagination run away with me."

"I can see why. We're all more than a little upset by what's happened."

"You can say that again. I still have trouble believing it. Where did you say we were going, by the way?"

"I didn't say. But we're going to Thompson's Crafts."

For just a second or two, Jack considered asking a silly question, like, "Are you going to buy a garden gnome?" But he restrained himself. He knew that Sally wouldn't do a thing like that. Would she?

"I want to talk to the Thompsons," Sally said, clarifying things. "I've been trying to get in touch with Tammi, but I haven't been able to reach her."

"Do you think they had something to do with Val's murder?" Jack asked.

"I don't know what to think." Sally told Jack about the forged purchase order. "I can't imagine why Val forged my name. And why would he buy all that material from the Thompsons, anyway?"

Jack could think of a reason immediately. "Blackmail. Val was messing around with Tammi Thompson, all right, and they were trying to profit from it."

Sally didn't say anything for a moment. She turned left, drove for a block, and turned left again. She stopped the car under a huge oak tree that shaded a long, barnlike tin building that had a hand-carved wooden sign in front. The sign's rustic letters spelled out "Thompson's Crafts."

She turned off the engine and said, "That doesn't make any sense. Tammi wouldn't turn Val in if she were trying to blackmail him."

Jack admitted that she had a point. He looked at the front window of the building and saw a black-and-white sign hanging there. In plain block letters, it said "CLOSED." Jack also saw a woman standing next to the window with her hand shading her eyes as she peered inside the building. She was surrounded by eight or nine concrete garden gnomes and birdbaths of various sizes.

"I can see why you couldn't get hold of the Thompsons," Jack said. "They aren't here."

"They aren't at home, either," Sally said. "I wonder what that woman is doing?"

"Trying to see if there's anyone in the building. Why don't we ask if she knows what's going on?"

"All right," Sally said, opening her door and stepping easily out of the car.

Jack's exit wasn't nearly so graceful. He had to unfold himself and then pull himself upright by holding onto the door. He was glad he had a sedan. It didn't look sporty, but it got him where he wanted to go. And he could get in and out without looking as if he were practicing for a yoga class.

The woman at the window turned to watch them as they approached her. She wasn't much taller than the largest of the concrete gnomes, and she was older than Jack had thought at first. In fact, she looked as if she might be somewhere in her eighties.

She was wearing a pair of wire-rimmed glasses with thick lenses. Her hair was dyed a light shade of orange, and she was wearing a yellow top and orange pants that didn't match the color of her hair at all.

"I don't understand why this place is closed," she said. "I've been trying to call all morning, but no one answered the phone. It's Wednesday, isn't it?"

Jack said that it was.

"Then why isn't the store open? There's no reason that it should be closed on a Wednesday. I need some silk flowers."

"We don't know why it's closed," Sally said. "We were hoping to talk to Mr. Thompson ourselves."

The woman pulled her glasses down on her nose and peered at Sally over the tops of the rims.

"I don't see why anyone would want to talk to him. I'd much rather deal with his wife. He's not a nice person at all."

Jack blinked and looked at Sally, who said, "He's not?"

"Oh, no. He has a terrible temper. I'd much rather go

somewhere else, but this is the only place in town that sells the things I want. And they took my car away from me last year, so I have to walk everywhere I go. It's a good thing I live near here."

"Has Mr. Thompson ever done anything to you?" Sally asked.

"Oh, no, not to me. He wouldn't dare. But you should hear the way he talks to his wife sometimes. If she makes any kind of mistake at all, like with the change, he's just terrible to her. He yells and carries on something awful. Why, one day, he threatened to hit her."

"You saw all that?"

The woman looked indignant. "Of course I did. I might not be able to drive, but I can see just fine. And I can hear, too, no matter what my daughter says."

"I'm sure you can," Sally said. "Did he actually hit her?"

"No, but he *threatened* to. He saw me and thought better of it. And I let him know what I thought of him, too, don't you think I didn't. I told him that in my day no decent man would dream of hitting a woman." She peered at Sally suspiciously. "It's all this women's lib stuff, is what it is. Men don't think women are anything special any more, and it's too bad if you ask me. My late husband always treated me with respect, and I didn't mind one little bit."

"I'm sure you didn't," Sally said, looking around for Jack, who had begun walking down the side of the building, looking in each of the small four-paned windows as he passed.

"That young man is going to get in trouble," the woman said. "Mr. Thompson has a real mean dog that he keeps in the back part of the store. If he's in there, he's liable to bite your friend."

"Not unless he can get inside," Sally said. "And I don't hear any barking."

The woman cocked her head. "Neither do I, come to think of it. Maybe the dog's not here, either."

There was a long sliding door near the back of the building, and Jack was shaking it. The shivering tin sounded vaguely like thunder.

"You'd better stop that," the woman called out. "Mr. Thompson will be awfully upset with you."

Jack wasn't worried about Mr. Thompson. He wanted to get inside and look around. He was getting a bad feeling about things. Maybe inside the building there would be some kind of clue as to the Thompsons' whereabouts.

Sally thought she knew what he was about to do, and she didn't think it was a good idea.

"Excuse me," she said to the woman, and left her standing there with the gnomes and birdbaths.

Sally walked toward the back of the building, kicking up little puffs of white dust from the caliche drive that ran along the side. Jack was still rattling the door when she got to him.

"What are you up to?" she said.

"I thought the door might be unlocked."

The door was held to the side of the building with a rusted iron hasp and secured by a fairly new padlock that Sally touched with her forefinger.

"Unlocked?" she said.

"Well, you never know about these things. That could be just for show."

Jack walked to the other end of the door. There was no hasp on that end, and Jack started pulling the door out from the wall. Because the door was old and loose, and because the end where Jack was standing was a good ten feet from the hasp, he easily created a crack at least a foot wide at the bottom. The door was on a track, so the crack narrowed as it approached the top.

"Jack," Sally said.

Jack ignored her and pulled a little harder. The crack widened considerably all the way up.

"See?" he said. "I told you it was unlocked."

And before she could say anything else, he slipped through the crack.

22

The inside of the building wasn't dark, but it wasn't exactly well lit, either. Jack smelled dust and dog food. Then he stumbled against a cardboard box, and something swatted him in the face.

He didn't yell, but he did jump backward and look around to see what had attacked him.

Then he yelled.

"What is it, Jack?" Sally asked.

She was standing at his elbow, and he pointed toward the object that had bumped him. Sally saw several evil faces leering at them. She also saw a couple of brightly colored burros covered in red and yellow paper, a sombrero, and even a couple of rocket ships.

"Piñatas," she said. "They're just piñatas."

Jack felt like a fool. "Well," he said, "they shouldn't hang them from the ceiling. A person could get hurt."

"I'm sure they're hung there for display purposes," Sally said.

Jack swallowed and tried to overcome his embarrassment. It wasn't as if he was afraid. He'd just been startled, that's all. He gave a closer look to his surroundings.

He was surprised to see that the floor of the building was the same white caliche as the drive outside. The Thompsons didn't put up much of a front.

As his eyes got more accustomed to the dim light, he saw a building full of things he neither needed nor wanted: paper flowers, imitation pot plants, pink plastic flamingos, plaster figures of dogs and cats, picture frames, knickknacks, bric-a-brac, *paddywack, give the dog a bone.*

"Stop it," he said aloud.

"Stop what?" Sally asked.

"Never mind. I was just going quietly crazy."

Jack noticed that everything was coated with a fine layer of dust, as if it had been there for quite some time without having sold. The Thompsons obviously weren't getting rich from their artsy-craftsy store. The idea of blackmail seemed more logical than before.

"I was never fond of places like this," Sally said. "What are we doing in here, anyway?"

"I don't know about you, but I was looking for clues."

"And I was just following you, to keep you out of trouble. We shouldn't be in here at all, you know. I wouldn't be a bit surprised if our little friend was calling the police right now."

"She'll have to get home first," Jack said. "And I'll bet she's still around. But you're right. We shouldn't be in here. There aren't any clues. Let's go."

He was shoving the door when Sally said, "Wait a minute, Jack."

"Why?" he said, letting the door slam back into place.

"Look over there."

Sally was pointing toward the back of the store where there

were no windows at all. It was quite murky there, but Jack thought he could see something dark outlined against the light-colored floor.

"It's probably nothing," he fibbed, not wanting to check it out.

Sally shook her head. "I think it's something. I'd better look."

Jack put a hand on her arm to restrain her.

"No," he said. "I'll do it."

Sally didn't try to stop him. Maybe the old woman's mini-lecture on the good old days before feminism had had an effect. Or maybe she just didn't want to see what was back there.

Because she was sure that what she could see was a person's arm, and if it was an arm, it was most likely going to be attached to a body.

Sally watched as Jack knelt down beside the arm. He was looking behind the boxes, and she could tell that he was being careful not to touch anything.

After a few seconds, he stood up and said, "You'd better come back here."

Sally took a step and then hesitated. "Is it . . . ?"

"I don't know who it is," Jack said. "But you might."

Sally forced herself to go forward. When she reached Jack's side, she looked down.

A woman was lying there, her face in the dust, her left arm outstretched. The hair on the back of her head was black with congealed blood, and there was blood on the caliche beside her. Flies buzzed busily around it.

"I'm not sure who it is," Sally said, feeling her stomach turn over. She thought it was Tammi Thompson, but she couldn't be positive. "I need to see her face."

"I don't think it would be a good idea to turn her over," Jack said. He was feeling queasy, and a cold sweat popped out on his face. "Do you want to make any guesses before we call the police?"

Sally's answer was cut off as a sudden clap of thunder rumbled through the building. To his credit, Jack didn't jump more than an inch or two, and he didn't yell. Neither did Sally.

"Someone's at the door," Jack said.

"And I hope it's not the police," Sally said. "I'd hate to be caught trespassing in a building where there's a dead body lying on the floor."

"Hey in there," the old woman yelled from outside. "I saw you go in. Open this door! I want my flowers."

"You can deal with her," Jack said. "I'll call the cops."

"No," Sally said. "You talk to her. See if you can get her to go home. I'll make the call. After all, the police in this town and I are practically on a first-name basis."

"Aren't they going to think it's a little odd, the way you keep stumbling over dead bodies?"

"I'm sure they are," Sally said. "That's why I want to be the one to call them."

"Be my guest," Jack said.

23

———

Sally stared at herself in the mirror. She was never at her best in the morning, and the sight of her hair always reminded her of a passage she'd read in graduate school. It was from the diary of Samuel Sewall, one of the last of the Puritans, who kept a daily record of his experiences, probably as a way of examining his life. When explaining to a friend why he refused to buy a wig, Sewall said he believed that God had given us our hair as a kind of test, to see if we could be content with it.

Sally had flunked the test many times. She had never been content with her hair, which also reminded her of another passage, this one from a more literary source, Shakespeare's sonnets: "If hairs be wires, then black wires grow upon her head."

No matter how many strokes she brushed it, no matter how many times she ran a comb through it, her hair sprang back into black tangles. Like her office, it was a hopeless case.

So she gave up on it and got out her pistol, intending to go to the range that afternoon. Then she gave Lola a kitty treat, for which she received small thanks, and left for school.

Detective Weems hadn't been pleased with her phone call the day before, and he was even less pleased when he arrived at Thompson's Crafts to discover that the body was that of Tammi Thompson.

Sally felt that she had to tell him about the forged purchase order. At first, that didn't make him feel any better.

But after Weems had thought about things for a minute, he'd changed his mind. In fact, he'd become positively cheerful, convinced that he now had the whole case well in hand.

"There's not much doubt about what happened," he said. "Thompson found out about his wife and Hurley, and he decided he could collect a little money by way of revenge, which might have worked if his wife hadn't squealed on Hurley. Thompson probably hadn't even told her about the blackmail angle, and then she screwed it up by complaining about Hurley. He lost his temper and killed her."

"What about Val?" she asked. "Why kill someone who's paying you money to keep quiet?"

"Principle," Weems said. "Hurley had been playing around with Thompson's wife, after all, and he probably wanted revenge. And now that she'd squealed, there wouldn't be any more money. Maybe he and Thompson even argued about it, and that's when Hurley got it."

Sally failed to see how Val's death would have been the result of someone's high principles, but she didn't want to get into a philosophical discussion with Weems. There were plenty of other things she didn't understand, either, but Weems wasn't going to talk about them with her. So she kept her mouth shut.

The woman who'd been looking inside the Thompsons' building didn't mind talking, however, and she and Weems discussed Ralph Thompson's violent tendencies at length.

Finally, Sally and Jack had been allowed to leave the building. They had gone back to the college and tried to conduct their business there in a more or less normal fashion. Sally didn't know how Jack had done in that regard, but she had felt odd for the rest of the day.

And she felt odd now, but for a different reason. She'd had strange dreams all night, probably caused by what she'd seen in the Thompsons' store.

It wasn't finding Tammi Thompson's body that she'd dreamed of, or even the faces of the piñatas that had hung suspended from the ceiling.

It was the picture frames.

The frames in the store had all been empty, waiting for someone to buy them and enclose a picture within their borders.

But the ones in Sally's dream hadn't been empty. They had all held pictures of goats with the number 666 engraved in their foreheads between their horns, and of course, they had all reminded her of the painting that was missing from the art gallery.

Sally couldn't seem to get the painting out of her head. She was convinced that it had something to do with the murders. Weems's explanation of what had happened made sense in a twisted way, and the detective might even have been correct in his assumptions.

Sally, however, didn't think so. She was virtually certain that the painting played a part in things, and yet there was really no way to connect the Thompsons to it.

Which meant that someone else had to be involved.

Who? Sally could think of only one person who might have a motive to take the painting: Roy Don Talon.

Sally realized that she wasn't a trained investigator. She knew that she could be completely wrong about Talon's possible involvement. However, she didn't like the idea of a puzzle with a missing piece that no one seemed interested in finding, so she felt that she had to do something to bring it to the attention of the police.

She parked her Acura in one of the few faculty spaces not occupied by cars with student stickers and went directly to Chief Desmond's office.

Geri Vale, who had been in one of Sally's classes a year or two previously, was the dispatcher. She was a short, stout blond woman who took everything very seriously.

"Is Chief Desmond in?" Sally asked.

"Yes," Geri said. "Do you need to see him?"

No, I was just checking up on him, Sally thought sarcastically. Then she said, "Yes, please."

Geri picked up her telephone and punched in four numbers. After a short wait, she said, "Dr. Good would like to talk to you, Chief." Then she listened and said, "All right."

She hung up the phone and told Sally to go right on back to the chief's office, which was one of three behind the dispatcher's area.

Desmond was looking spiffy, as usual. He was wearing a dark suit with a bright white shirt and a red patterned tie. He stood up when Sally entered, and she couldn't see a wrinkle anywhere, not in the suit and not in Desmond's face.

"Good morning, Dr. Good," he said. "What can the HCC police do for you today?"

"You can tell me what you've found out about the painting that's missing from the art gallery," Sally said.

Desmond laughed and asked her to have a seat. "I can see you're still concerned about that. But you shouldn't be. Not after what happened yesterday."

He looked at Sally. "Yes, I've talked to Detective Weems, and he told me all about your finding another body. But he says the case is all tied up in a neat bundle now. He says that the killer is Ralph Thompson. It's just a matter of tracking him down. And I have to say that I agree with him."

Sally sat in a chair across the desk from Desmond. "How can you be so sure?"

"The killer's M.O.," Desmond said. "It's the same in both cases."

Sally didn't ask what an M.O. was, and Desmond looked vaguely disappointed.

"The victims were both struck by heavy objects," Desmond said after a couple of seconds.

Sally hadn't seen any heavy objects near Tammi Thompson, so she asked Desmond how he knew.

"Things like that are easy to tell if you're a professional," Desmond said. "I'm sure the autopsy will bear me out."

"But the statue that was used on Val Hurley was lying right there beside him. There was nothing near Tammi, so the M.O.'s not the same."

Desmond looked irritated. "There's not that much difference. Thompson probably realized that he'd made a mistake the first time, so he took the weapon with him."

"And now the investigation is closed?"

"We really didn't have much to do with it in the first place," Desmond said. "Our part was finished when Weems took over. But that doesn't mean it's closed. It won't be closed until they catch up with Thompson."

"What about Roy Don Talon?"

Desmond, who had been slumping a little in his chair, snapped to attention.

"It wouldn't be a good idea to drag him into this," he said.

"Why not?"

"Because he had nothing to do with it, that's why."

"You don't know that. What other explanation is there for the missing painting?"

"I don't have to know anything, and I don't have to tie in the painting. Weems is sure about Thompson, and that's all that matters."

Sally stood up. Then she glanced down at Desmond's desk, which was much neater than her own, of course. But that just made it easier to see the piece of paper lying there.

It was the page that Desmond had taken from the guest register in the art gallery, and Sally saw that the last two names were those of Ellen Baldree and Jorge Rodriguez. They had been the last two people in the art gallery on the day that Val had been killed—or at least they had been the last to sign their names in the register.

Sally thought about what Jack had told her, and she thought about her conversation with Ellen. Both of them would be considered suspects in Val's murder if the police had been doing a proper investigation.

She took another peek, trying to see if A. B. D. Johnson's name was anywhere on the list.

Desmond saw what she was looking at, picked up the paper, and put it in a drawer.

"That's not important anymore, either," he said.

Sally didn't bother to comment. It was time for her to go to class.

Before she left Desmond's office, he said, "The college will be closing this afternoon at one for Val's funeral. There should be a notice in everyone's mailbox. You should probably tell your students."

"I'll do that," Sally said.

She left the chief's office and went down the hallway to her favorite classroom, the one that no one else liked because it was located near an air vent and was quite noisy. It was also considered too big by most of the other instructors.

Sally didn't mind the noise or the size. She liked the room because it wasn't on the main part of the hallway, so she wasn't likely to be disturbed by other instructors or their students.

Sally's own students were unusually attentive, especially

when they learned that the college would be closing early and that they could skip their afternoon classes.

Besides being attentive, most of the students had actually read the assignment. There was a lively discussion about the use of what the O. J. Simpson trial had taught the world to call the "*n* word" in Sherwood Anderson's "I'm a Fool." One student thought the story should be excluded from all textbooks and possibly banned from publication anywhere, forever. None of Sally's arguments about freedom of speech, literary values, or characterization in the story could change his mind.

Aside from that, however, the class was uneventful, something that couldn't be said for the rest of the day. It would become known around the HCC campus as the day A. B. D. Johnson finally went ballistic.

24

It happened in the faculty mailroom just as Sally was walking by the half-open door. There were usually only a few people in there between classes: those who'd come to check their mail, those who were buying a Dr. Pepper from the faculty association's soft-drink machine, and those who were passing through on their way to use the restrooms in the faculty lounge.

And of course there were always a few of the part-time instructors, like Coy Webster, who was the one A. B. D. Johnson attacked.

Sally heard the commotion when she was a couple of yards from the door. By the time she reached it and went inside, Coy was lying on the floor, a dented mailbasket beside him and campus-mail envelopes scattered all around.

A. B. D. was standing over Coy, breathing heavily. He picked up the mailbasket and was about to give Coy another good whack when Troy Beauchamp, who was standing beside A. B. D., grabbed the basket, jerked it out of A. B. D.'s hands, and set it on the counter behind them.

"Are you crazy?" Troy asked.

A. B. D. glared at him. "Don't look at me! It's not my fault that everyone's out to get me. Fieldstone's going to fire me if he gets half an excuse, and now that cretin"—he pointed to a quivering Coy Webster—"is telling everyone I was in the art gallery before Val was killed!"

Coy Webster didn't appear to have been injured, but Sally nevertheless felt sorry for him. He was short and thin and wore clothes that looked as if he found them in thrift stores and couldn't be too picky about the fit. His scrawny legs stuck out the ends of his pants, and his socks drooped down around his ankles, covering the tops of his scuffed brown shoes. His faded shirt hung on him like a muumuu.

Sally put her books down on the table that sat in the middle of the mailroom and bent to help Coy get up. Troy restrained A. B. D.

"So, what were you saying about the art gallery?" Sally asked.

"N-nothing," Coy replied, rising gingerly and moving so that the table was between him and A. B. D. "I wasn't saying a thing."

"Yes, he was," Troy said. "He was telling me that A. B. D. was hanging around the Art and Music Building late yesterday."

"So what if I was?" A. B. D. said. "I have every right to be there if I want to!"

"Coy says there was a lot of yelling going on in Val's office," Troy said.

He tightened his grip on A. B. D., who was looking longingly at the mailbasket.

"I-I'm not sure about what I heard," Coy said. "I could be mistaken."

"And what was *he* doing there, anyway?" A. B. D. asked. "Doesn't anyone want to know that? I'll bet he was skulking around Val's office, just waiting for his chance to off him. Ask him that! Go ahead and ask him!"

Off him? Sally thought. A. B. D. had probably been watching too many old TV shows. Or maybe he hadn't watched any TV since the sixties. That seemed more likely.

"Why would Coy want to off—kill Val?" Sally asked.

"Because Coy was sleeping in that building illegally, that's why," A. B. D. said.

"What?" Sally said, though she wasn't surprised, considering what Douglas Young had told her the day before.

"It's true," Troy said. "I've known for a week."

Sally looked at Coy, who looked away, but not before he nodded.

"Why didn't you tell me?" Sally asked Troy.

"I didn't think it was that important. There are some things that a division chair shouldn't be bothered about."

"Coy?" Sally said. "Since I'm already being bothered, why don't you tell me what was going on?"

Coy still didn't look in her direction, preferring to stare at the nearly colorless toes of his shoes.

"I've separated from my wife," he said. "I didn't have enough money to stay in a motel, so I thought I might find a place somewhere around here. There's no one in those art labs at night, so I stayed there. I didn't bother anyone or touch any of the art equipment. I've been showering in the gym in the mornings."

"But what about your other teaching jobs?" Sally asked.

"This is a sort of central location," Coy said. "I've been able to get to them more easily than when I was at home, actually."

"Who cares about how he gets to his jobs?" A. B. D. asked. "What does that have to do with anything? He killed Val, and now he's trying to blame me."

"You were there in his office," Coy said. "You were yelling."

A. B. D. twisted out of Troy's grasp and grabbed the mailbasket. He raised it over his head, prepared to strike.

"All right, I was there. I was trying to get Val to admit that he didn't need that new chair! And he didn't!"

Troy made a grab for the basket, but A. B. D. danced away. Troy banged his knee against the table and hopped around holding it. Just then, Eric Desmond came through the door. It didn't take him long to size things up.

"Drop the basket, Johnson," he said.

A. B. D. obeyed immediately. The basket clonked on the floor at his feet.

"I had three instructors and five students beating down my door about a fight in here," Desmond said. "What the hell's going on?"

Sally explained as quickly as she could. A. B. D. scowled at her the whole time, while Coy stared at his shoes.

"I think we'd better go down to my office," Desmond said.

Troy stopped hopping around and limped over to join them.

"Not you, Beauchamp," Desmond said. "Don't you have a class to teach?"

"As a matter of fact," Troy said, "I don't."

"Well, go translate some Chaucer then," Desmond said. "The rest of you, come with me."

Sally was the last one out of the mailroom. She looked back over her shoulder at Troy, who was clearly crushed at being excluded from the juiciest session of the year. Nothing pained him more than to think that there was something going on that he didn't know about.

"Tell me what happens," he called after Sally, who smiled, shrugged, and let the door swing shut behind her.

25

I don't think there's any law against sleeping in the campus buildings," Desmond said after both A. B. D. and Webster had told their stories and he had asked them a number of questions. "As long as it doesn't happen again, we'll overlook it. And as for what just went on in the mailroom, I think we can just forget it ever happened, unless Mr. Webster wants to file some kind of complaint, which I'm sure he doesn't. Right, Mr. Webster?"

Coy nodded vigorously. "Right."

"And I'm sure Mr. Johnson regrets what happened and will make sure nothing like it ever happens again. Right, Mr. Johnson?"

A. B. D. wasn't nearly as enthusiastic as Coy had been. In fact, he looked downright recalcitrant, and it didn't appear that he was going to answer.

Desmond said again, "Right, Mr. Johnson?" in a tone implying that recalcitrance would not be tolerated.

A. B. D. took a deep breath, let it out slowly, and finally answered, "Right."

"Good." Desmond said, with a smile that didn't show even a hint of teeth. "Now, why don't we all get back to our jobs and quit frightening the students? They might get the idea that it's not safe to go to school here, and we wouldn't want that. After all, they pay our salaries."

Coy and A. B. D. stood up. Sally, who couldn't believe what was happening, didn't move.

"You two go on and get out of here," Desmond said to Coy and A. B. D. "I want to talk to Dr. Good."

Coy hung back until A. B. D. had cleared the doorway; then he followed him reluctantly.

When they were gone, Sally said to Desmond, "Would you mind telling me what's going on here?"

"Problem solving," Desmond replied with another of his thin smiles. "Those two had a problem, and I solved it. They might not be the best of friends, but you can be sure there won't be any more fighting."

Sally had seen the word *flabbergasted* in print numerous times, but she'd never truly understood what it meant until that moment.

"Fighting? You're worried about fighting? What about murder? Those two were admittedly in the art gallery late yesterday afternoon. A. B. D. was yelling at Val, and there was an angry scene. Don't you think you should investigate a little more thoroughly?"

Desmond leaned back in his chair. He didn't appear to have a worry in the world. It was as if Val's murder had never happened, or, if it had, it was now solved and there was no need to discuss it further.

"You heard what Webster said. There was a commotion, sure, but after that, Johnson left the building. There was no scuffle, no noise of any other kind. Johnson didn't kill Hurley."

"Did Coy check to see?" Sally asked. Then she answered

herself. "He says he didn't. So how do you know what happened in that office?"

"I don't know," Desmond said, unconcerned. "But I can draw an inference. No noise, no scuffle, equals no dead man."

"A. B. D. could have come back later, when Coy wasn't there," Sally said. "For that matter, what about Coy? He could have killed Val to keep Val from telling anyone that Coy was sleeping in the building."

"We don't even know that Hurley knew what Coy was doing. And if he did, it would be crazy to kill someone to keep it a secret. Webster's a little weird, I'll give you that, and his clothes are terrible, but he's not crazy. And, as I've said before, this isn't my investigation. It's Weems's job now."

Desmond smiled his thin smile as if to say there was no use in continuing the conversation.

But Sally wasn't going to give up that easily. She had a lot more to say.

"What if Coy knows more than he's telling? What if someone else was in that building and Coy knows it?"

Desmond sighed. "He just sat right here and told us his story. You heard him. He says that he had an evening class on another campus last night. He left around four-thirty so he could get a hamburger on the way."

"Someone went into that building and took the painting of the goat," Sally said. "Have you forgotten about that?"

"I told you earlier today not to worry about the painting. We don't know that anyone took it, but even if someone did, there's no connection with Val's death."

Sally didn't try to conceal her amazement. "You can't be sure of that. The murder might be Weems's job, but the painting's yours."

Desmond leaned forward, no longer relaxed. He wasn't smiling now.

"Are you trying to tell me that I don't know how to do my job?" he asked.

"No," Sally said. "I'm sure you're very good at your job. But I don't understand how you can just ignore what Coy's told you about A. B. D. And I don't see how you can say that the painting doesn't have anything to do with Val's murder. It seems to me that it most certainly does, and I think you should report it to Detective Weems. If it's his job, he should have this new information."

"You don't have to worry about that," Desmond said.

Sally thought that you didn't have to be an English teacher to hear the ambiguity in that statement.

"Especially the part about the painting," she said.

"Why?" Desmond asked.

"Well," Sally said, and then she paused, because she really didn't have an answer.

Desmond relaxed again. "You see what I mean? If the painting's gone, and I'm not saying that it is, anyone could have taken it. A faculty member who admired it, a student who thought it would look good in his apartment, anybody."

Sally thought about it. Desmond had a point, but there were some possibilities he hadn't mentioned.

What about an administrator who didn't want the painting to cause any more trouble?

What about a certain car dealer who suddenly changed his mind and decided the jury picked to decide the artwork's fate would not be fair? What if he then thought he'd show the painting to his own handpicked jury?

What might have happened if either the administrator or the car dealer had gotten into an argument with Val? Would someone have lost his temper?

It seemed likely to Sally, but it was obvious that, other than she herself, no one cared.

Well, if Desmond wouldn't investigate, she'd just have to

do something about it on her own. She wasn't afraid of Roy Don Talon, no matter how much money he paid in taxes, and she didn't want to see Ralph Thompson take the blame for the murders of Val and Tammi if he wasn't the killer. Everyone else seemed quite happy to do that, however.

Desmond looked at her as if he were reading her mind.

"You wouldn't be considering doing any more meddling, would you?" he said. "You've already caused enough trouble around here. Stumbling over dead bodies isn't exactly the way to get in good with the administration."

"I'm not trying to get in good with anyone," Sally said. "I'm just trying to get people to do their jobs."

"I'll do my job," Desmond said. He stood up. "Weems will do his. You do yours, and we'll all be happy."

Sally didn't like being dismissed, but she didn't see any point in talking to Desmond any longer. He wasn't going to listen. She stood up and smiled at him.

"You don't have to worry about me," she said. "I'll stay out of your way."

Desmond didn't look as if he believed her, but he said, "That's good. I'm sure that's the way Dr. Fieldstone would want it."

Sally saw that as an implied threat, but she didn't say anything. She just turned and left the office.

She could feel Desmond's eyes on her back all the way out.

26

Sally went to her office, sat down, and stared glumly at the student papers strewn over her desk. She really needed to grade them. Her students were beginning to wonder if they were ever going to get them back.

But Sally couldn't get her mind off the murders. She could understand the way Weems and Desmond were thinking; Ralph Thompson, enraged by what had happened, killed his wife and then went to the school and killed Val.

Or vice versa.

That was the simple answer. It tied everything up in a neat package and gave the investigation one person to concentrate on. But it bothered Sally that Weems and Desmond were ignoring all kinds of important things, of which the missing painting was only one.

Some of them she hadn't even mentioned to Desmond.

There was the forged purchase order, for example. She hadn't wanted to tell Weems about it, but she had.

Then there were those signatures showing that Ellen Baldree and Jorge Rodriguez had visited the art gallery. Either one of them could have gotten into an argument with Val, Ellen over past grievances or Jorge over current ones. And the argument could have gotten out of hand.

Coy Webster might know. Sally was almost sure he was hiding something, though she had no idea what it was.

Not that she blamed him for not wanting to talk about it. His position at HCC was far from secure, just like his position in the rest of his life. He was probably regretting ever having said anything to Troy Beauchamp, but he shouldn't blame himself for that. Troy was a master of worming information out of people, even those with more gumption than Coy.

Sally was about to reach for a Hershey bar when the telephone rang. She picked it up and answered.

"Please hold for Dr. Fieldstone," said Eva Dillon.

"Shit," Sally said.

"I beg your pardon?"

"Sorry, Eva. I didn't mean anything personal."

Eva laughed quietly. "I know. I'll put Dr. Fieldstone on."

There was a short wait, and Dr. Fieldstone said, "Dr. Good?"

A bad sign, of course. Fieldstone wasn't in a good mood. Sally was having a strong feeling of déjà vu.

"Yes?" she said.

"Could you please come over to my office for a moment?"

The feeling of déjà vu got stronger. After the two meetings in Desmond's office, Sally was beginning to feel like the soldier in *Catch-22*, the one who saw everything twice.

"Of course," she said. "I'll be there in ten minutes."

"Thank you," Dr. Fieldstone said, and hung up.

"Shit," Sally said again.

This time, there was no one else in Fieldstone's office. He stood up when Sally came in and asked her to take a seat.

"And then we can have a talk," he said.

Sally didn't like the way he was avoiding her eyes, but she sat down and waited to see what he had to say.

Instead of sitting down himself, Fieldstone walked around to the front of his desk and sat on the edge of it. The casual approach. He didn't look comfortable, but Sally couldn't tell whether that was because of his position or because of what he wanted to talk to her about.

"I believe you have some idea that our police department isn't up to the job of investigating Val Hurley's murder," he said finally.

Sally wasn't sure which police department he meant.

"Local or campus?" she asked.

"I'm referring to Eric Desmond."

So now Sally knew who'd ratted her out.

She said, "As I understand it, they aren't part of the investigation. That's up to the local police."

"But I also have reason to believe you suspect that Detective Weems is on the wrong track."

Sally didn't know what to say, so she just kept her mouth shut.

Fieldstone tried to wait her out, but he didn't have a chance. Sally had waited out students for much longer periods of silence than Fieldstone could ever tolerate.

"Desmond and Weems know what they're doing," Fieldstone finally said. He pushed himself away from the desk and stood in front of her. "They're accomplished professionals, and they have access to certain . . . facts that you don't know. So I hope you'll let them do their jobs and not interfere."

Why was everyone so sure she would interfere? Sally wondered. Did they all think of her as some dangerously meddlesome woman?

"I know that some things seem hard to understand right

now," Fieldstone went on. "But I'm sure that later on they'll all become clear."

Sally didn't get it. Was Fieldstone implying that there was some complicated plot that she didn't know about?

Fieldstone tried perching on the desk again, but the casual look didn't suit him at all.

"There are certain . . . matters that could have some effect on the school's reputation," he said. "I'm sure you understand what I mean."

Sally thought it was time to say something, so she told him that she didn't understand at all.

"I'm sure you don't," Fieldstone said, contradicting what he'd said five seconds before. Maybe he'd been secretly reading Walt Whitman. "But whether you understand or not doesn't matter. You can be sure that everything is under control. Do you see what I'm getting at?"

This time Sally thought she did. "You're saying that I shouldn't be questioning things."

"Oh, no. Not at all. I wouldn't dream of interfering with your freedom of speech. I hope you don't think that."

Sally certainly did think that, and she was determined not to make things easy on Fieldstone.

"It sounds that way to me," she said.

"Well, it shouldn't. I wish I could say more, but at the moment I really can't. You do know that you can trust me, don't you?"

Sally smiled, knowing what someone like A. B. D. Johnson would think about trusting an administrator.

"Of course I trust you," she lied.

Fieldstone looked relieved. "Fine. Fine. I knew you'd understand. I'm glad we had this little talk."

Sally had lost count of how many times Fieldstone had reversed his field, but she knew it didn't matter. Their "little talk" had done the opposite of what Fieldstone had hoped. It had made her even more certain than ever that something funny was going on. She just wished she could figure out what it was.

She started to get up, but Fieldstone waved her back to her chair.

"We're not finished," he said. "Someone else is going to join us."

He picked up his phone, pressed a button, and said, "Ms. Dillon, could you send Ms. Willis and Dean Naylor in?"

Shit, Sally thought.

27

D ean Naylor ushered Amy Willis into Fieldstone's office. While Naylor looked as calm and suave as ever, Amy looked even worse than she had the last time Sally had seen her. She was a bundle of twitches, and her hair was wild. Her clothes looked as if she might have put them on after washing them and then giving them no more than a couple of minutes in the "air fluff" cycle.

Naylor got Amy into a chair, where she crossed and un-crossed her legs four times before Naylor even had time to greet Sally. Sally didn't blame Amy for her nervousness. She was about to get scorched, if she hadn't been already, for the five-thousand-dollar purchase order.

Fieldstone didn't go for the casual approach this time. He sat behind his desk, looking as serious as a federal judge, and took the P.O. from a desk drawer.

After staring at it for a second or two, he said, "What can you tell me about this, Ms. Willis?"

Amy patted her hair, shifted in the chair, and finally said, "I don't know what to tell you about it."

Dean Naylor smiled. "Why don't you just tell us how it slipped by you?"

Amy looked at Sally, who wished that she could help. But there was nothing she could do. Amy was on her own.

"It was all in order," Amy said, sounding as if she didn't believe it for a minute. Her right leg was crossed over her left, and her left foot was beating out a jazzy rhythm on the carpet.

"But five thousand dollars?" Naylor said.

Amy tried to smooth her hair. It didn't work. Sally could sympathize.

"I've already explained all this to Dr. Good," Amy said. "And then I talked to Mr. Wistrom."

Wistrom was the school's business manager. Sally wondered why he wasn't there.

"Mr. Wistrom says that he didn't know a thing about this," Fieldstone said.

Ah-ha, Sally thought. *Keep your distance. Maintain plausible deniability. Not a bad strategy.* Well, since Wistrom was out of it, she might as well give everyone a little surprise.

"The police know," Sally announced, and Amy nearly jumped out of her chair. She turned startlingly pale, and Sally thought she might faint. Even Naylor looked stunned.

Fieldstone was the only one of them able to speak. "Who told them?" he asked, although it was clear from the way he looked at Sally that he already had a good idea of the answer.

So Sally confessed.

"I did, when they were questioning me about Tammi Thompson's murder. I thought there might be some connection, so it seemed like the right thing to do."

At the mention of Tammi Thompson's death, Amy got even paler, though Sally wouldn't have thought it was possible.

Naylor was agitated. He obviously didn't agree that telling

the police was the right thing to do.

"What did they think about it?" he asked.

"They seemed to think it explains a lot. To them, it means that Ralph Thompson was blackmailing Val."

"Why would he kill someone who was providing him with money?" Naylor asked.

Sally smiled. "That's a very good question."

"But I'm sure Weems had an answer," Fieldstone said.

"Oh, yes. They think that Tammi didn't know about the blackmail when she complained to the school about Val."

"Ah," Naylor said. "So her husband killed her because she spoiled his little scheme."

"That's close enough," Sally said. "But why did he kill Val?"

"Because Val had offended his sense of honor," Fieldstone replied.

Sally felt as if she had fallen down a rabbit hole or wandered through the looking glass. Blackmailers and killers were honorable? Well, it wasn't that far removed from what Weems thought, but it still didn't make sense to her.

Amy, however, was nodding vigorously as if it were a brilliant deduction. Sally wondered if everyone needed a short course in logic.

"Back to this purchase order," Fieldstone said, rattling the paper to get everyone's attention. "Ms. Willis tells me that these signatures are forged."

"I can only speak for mine," Sally said, though she was certain the others were forged as well.

"That's not my signature," Naylor said, not even glancing at the paper.

"Nor mine," Fieldstone said. "Yet Ms. Willis didn't notice that. She simply had a check cut for Ralph Thompson's shop."

"I didn't cut the check," Amy said, sliding from one side of the chair to the other.

"But you sent the order through."

Amy sniffled loudly and brushed at her eyes with the back of her hand. Naylor pulled a sparkling white handkerchief from his pocket and handed it to her.

Leave it to Naylor to carry a handkerchief, Sally thought.

Amy took the handkerchief and dried her eyes. Then she started twisting it in her hands. Sally watched as it got smaller and smaller.

"Yes," Amy said at last. "I sent it through. That's my job. All the required signatures were there, and I thought that was good enough."

"How did Hurley ever think he could get away with it?" Fieldstone asked no one in particular. "He must have known we'd find out what he'd done."

Amy said, "That's what I wanted . . . want to know. After I'd thought about it for a while, I knew there had to be a mistake. I just waited too long to figure that out."

She started crying again, snuffling into the remains of Naylor's handkerchief.

"I think this has gone on long enough," Sally said. "Amy made a mistake, and she realizes it. There's no need to humiliate her."

"We weren't trying to humiliate her," Naylor said, as if surprised that anyone would suggest such a thing. "We were just trying to find out what happened."

"Well," Sally said, "now you know."

"Yes," Fieldstone said. "A mistake. A five-thousand-dollar mistake. This isn't going to look good to the Board."

"Please," Amy said, her voice cracking. "Please, don't fire me. I'm a single mother. If I lose my job, I don't know what I'll do!"

Sally knew enough about Amy's situation to know that Amy's former husband would have taken custody of their six-year-old son in a heartbeat, but she didn't say anything. There was no need to give Fieldstone more of an advantage than he already had.

Instead, she said, "Val's the one who defrauded the college, and there's nothing you can do to him. Besides, I'm sure the school has insurance."

"That's true," Naylor said. "But we can't just overlook something like this."

"You've overlooked other things," Sally said, taking a chance. "Right now, you're overlooking the fact that there's a painting missing from the art gallery."

Naylor and Fieldstone exchanged glances. Amy was crying too hard to notice, but Sally did. Naylor put his hand on Amy's shoulder.

"There's no need to cry," he said. "This will all be taken care of. We'll have to put a note in your personnel file, of course, and if anything like it happens again, then termination will certainly be an option. But for now, why don't you just take the rest of the day off and come in tomorrow for a fresh start?"

Amy had wadded the handkerchief into a knot about the size of a golf ball. She started to unfold it and smooth it on her thighs. Her shoulders still shook with sobbing.

"Are you s-sure that would be a-all right?" she asked.

"Of course," Naylor said. "And keep the handkerchief. You might need it again."

Amy stood up, passing the damp handkerchief from hand to hand. Then she wiped her face with it and said, "Thank you. I'll be more careful in the future."

"I'm sure you will," Fieldstone said, standing.

Naylor stood, too, and patted Amy on the shoulder as he guided her to the door. When she was gone, both men sat back down and looked at Sally.

"We won't be discussing the painting anymore," Fieldstone said. "Chief Desmond is on the job, and anything we say about it might jeopardize his investigation. You shouldn't have brought it up in front of Ms. Willis."

Desmond hadn't sounded to Sally as if he was doing any heavy investigation.

"I'm sorry," she said.

"What I don't understand is how Ms. Willis could have made such a mistake," Naylor said. "She's usually the most conscientious person in the Business Office. Nothing gets by her."

"I know," Fieldstone said. He put the P.O. back into the desk drawer. "That's probably why she's so upset. It's the first mistake she's ever made."

"I'm sure she's made errors before," Naylor said. "It's just that she's been able to deal with them before they came to our attention."

"Yes. Well, it's too bad she wasn't able to do that this time. The Board won't be happy, and I'm sure the newspaper will have a field day."

"If anyone there finds out," Naylor said.

"Yes," Fieldstone said. He smiled slightly. He was good at keeping secrets, and Naylor was even better. "There's that. The reporter who does the articles on our board meetings is pretty nosy, however. She always asks a lot of questions."

Both men looked at Sally.

"I had to tell the police," she said. "I thought it might have something to do with Tammi Thompson's death. But I don't have to tell anyone else."

"Good," Fieldstone said. "Of course, it's a matter of public record. It might even show up in the police report, though I doubt it. Still, anyone could find out about the purchase order by looking in the right place."

"Purchase order?" Naylor said.

"What purchase order?" Sally said.

Fieldstone smiled.

28

Jack Neville spent most of the day playing Minesweeper. He'd managed to achieve his best time ever at the expert level, but he didn't feel any elation.

Seeing Val lying dead on the floor of his office had been bad enough, but there was something even worse about discovering the body of one of the college's students in the dusty back end of the Thompsons' craft store. He was still very upset.

And now Jack was going to have to go to Val's funeral. He hated funerals. He couldn't think of a single good thing about them. He didn't like the music, he didn't like the platitudes, he didn't like the flowers, and he didn't like trying to comfort the mourners because he never knew what to say to them.

In Val's case, of course, there wouldn't be much of a problem with mourners. Val didn't have many close friends on the faculty, unless you counted the women he'd dated, and there were plenty of those. Jack wasn't sure any of them would be mourning, however. Val had been a love-'em-and-leave-'em sort of guy.

And Val didn't have a family. He'd never married, he had no brothers or sisters, and his parents had died years earlier.

But, mourners or not, all the other trappings of the funeral would be there, and Jack would have preferred to avoid them. Thank goodness he hadn't been asked to be one of the pall-bearers, as several other faculty members had been.

Since he didn't have any official functions to perform, he didn't even have to go to the funeral, he told himself. But attendance was pretty much expected of the faculty, so he would grit his teeth and go. Besides, he wanted to talk to Sally about a new theory he'd developed. It seemed quite logical to him, and it explained a lot of different things.

Of course, he'd developed the theory while playing Mine-sweeper, so it might not hang together. And his earlier theory hadn't seemed very inspired when he'd told Sally about it. That's why he needed to discuss the new one with her, to put it to the test.

Or that's what he tried to tell himself. He knew there was more to it than that. In fact, he'd probably developed the theory just so he'd have an excuse to talk to her. If he'd really thought it was the solution to the murders, he would have told the police.

Wouldn't he? He wasn't sure.

He looked at his watch. It was almost time to leave for the funeral.

But he could probably work in one more game of Mine-sweeper.

Jack talked himself out of the game, and feeling virtuous and proud of himself, he got to the church a little early. It wasn't crowded when he arrived, but he sat in the back row anyway. Val was in the open casket down at the front, and Jack didn't want to sit any closer than he had to.

A. B. D. Johnson was already seated, silently fulminating a couple of rows in front of Jack. A. B. D.'s head nodded slowly from side to side as if A. B. D. were keeping time with the anguished sound of the organ.

Not far from A. B. D. sat Coy Webster in a suit that looked as if it had been packed away in a trunk for about seven years and brought out fifteen minutes before Coy put it on. Coy looked a little as if he'd been kept in a trunk himself.

Just in front of them sat Amy Willis, whose wild hair exploded from her head in all directions. Jack caught a glimpse of a yellow pencil sticking in it. Amy wasn't nodding her head so much as twitching her whole body. As Jack watched, he became certain that the trembling wasn't voluntary. Amy was always nervous, but maybe funerals made her even more jittery than usual.

Then Jack spotted Sally Good sitting about five rows in front of him. She was alone, and Jack wondered if she would mind having company—specifically, *his* company—even if it wasn't exactly comforting her that he had in mind.

Telling himself that it was really shameful to have such thoughts at a funeral, he got up and moved.

Sally smiled at him when he sat down, and he immediately felt better. Maybe the funeral wouldn't be so bad after all, even though the organ was mourning its tortuous way through a particularly lugubrious hymn.

"Was Val a regular churchgoer?" Jack whispered, just loud enough to be heard above the sound of the organ.

"I don't know," Sally whispered back. "But somehow I doubt it."

Jack doubted it, too.

"I'd like to talk to you after the service," Jack said. "I have an idea about Tammi and Val."

"What is it?"

"It's kind of complicated. Are you going to the cemetery?"

"No."

"We can talk in the hall, then."

Sally nodded. "All right."

The church began to fill up, and Jack didn't say any more. President Fieldstone came in and sat near the front. Dean Naylor was with him. They both looked as solemn as Puritan divines at a witchcraft trial.

Vera Vaughn walked down the aisle between Ellen Baldree and Jorge Rodriguez. Vera was dry-eyed, and Jack thought that some women certainly did look good in black, even if it wasn't black leather. Ellen seemed vaguely unhappy, but she wasn't openly grieving, though Jack knew that she'd dated Val for a while.

Jorge looked stoic, which Jack didn't find surprising. After all, Jorge was by all accounts no stranger to violent death. And he was being quite attentive to Vera, which Jack found interesting.

Then the pallbearers came in, and the service began. It wasn't as bad as Jack had feared. The minister obviously hadn't known Val well, if at all, and no one from the college had volunteered to give a eulogy. As a result, the minister didn't seem to think that a lengthy sermon was necessary. So the service was as short and unemotional as it was possible for a funeral to be. Even the hymns weren't too dismal.

When the service was over and people were filing out behind the casket, there were a few more tears than there had been earlier. People hadn't been entirely unaffected by Val's untimely passing. Ellen Baldree, in particular, was visibly upset.

Jack couldn't figure out why, since there hadn't been anything said or done to bring out the tears. Maybe he was being too cynical. Maybe she had genuinely cared for Val, and the fact of his loss was just now sinking in.

As soon as she reached the narthex, Ellen pushed through the crowd and headed for the restroom, followed closely by Vera Vaughn. Jorge stood back, staring after them, looking as perplexed as Jack felt.

"I'll be back in a minute," Sally said, leaving Jack to follow Ellen and Vera.

"What happened?" Jack asked Jorge.

Jorge shrugged. "I don't know. She seemed fine until the very end of the service. Then she just broke down. Maybe it was the prayer."

Jack thought about it. He couldn't recall anything in the prayer that was particularly upsetting.

"Or maybe it was singing 'Amazing Grace,' " Jorge said. "That one always gets to me."

It always got to Jack, too, but not in the way something had gotten to Ellen. He was tempted to boldly go where no man had gone before, into the women's restroom, just to see what he could find out. But he decided that it would be better to trust Sally for that.

He hoped she wouldn't be long.

29

Sally let the restroom door hiss shut behind her. Vera Vaughn was standing beside Ellen, who was at the sink, splashing cold water on her face.

"Hello, Vera," Sally said.

Vera nodded. Her hair didn't move, though it didn't appear to have any kind of spray, gel, or mousse on it at all. It was just naturally lustrous, and Sally supposed that Vera made it stay in place by sheer willpower. Vera would be an easy person to hate.

"Is Ellen all right?" Sally asked.

Vera nodded again. This time, Sally thought she saw a single hair move. Not much, admittedly, but nevertheless it did move. It made Sally feel a little better about Vera. Not much, but a little.

"Is there anything I can do to help?"

"I don't believe so," Vera said. "Ellen is fine."

Ellen didn't seem fine to Sally. She was looking in the mirror and crying. Tears and water dripped down her face, and her makeup was ruined.

"I'll get some paper towels," Sally said.

She went to the dispenser and pulled out about two feet of toweling. She was sure the church's tithers could afford it. She handed it to Ellen, who reached back and took it without looking away from the mirror.

When she had a firm grip on the toweling, Ellen wadded it up in her hands and started to rub her face, while Vera looked on in vague amusement.

"I didn't want to make a scene," Ellen snuffled. "I tried not to break down."

"Women are conditioned to weep at funerals," Vera said. "It's cultural, and it's a hard thing to overcome. You'll notice that men never cry."

Sally didn't think this was strictly true, and she noticed that Vera didn't seem to be having any difficulty restraining her own tears.

"It's just that it's so sad," Ellen said.

She looked down at the toweling in her hand. It was wet and covered with makeup, and after a little further wadding, she threw it in the trash can.

"It's not really sad at all," Vera said. "Val's bad habits just caught up with him."

"What bad habits?" asked Sally.

Vera gave her a surprised glance. "You mean you don't know?"

"Of course she doesn't know," Ellen said. "She doesn't know anything that goes on around the school. For all she knows about what's happening, she might as well be teaching somewhere else. Like Kathmandu."

Sally didn't take offense. She knew that Ellen didn't like her and had no respect for her abilities as a division chair. Besides, it appeared that she was simply telling the truth.

"Maybe I'd know more if people would let me in on their secrets," she said.

Vera smiled crookedly. "Isn't this the picture of femininity? Here were are, exchanging secrets in the ladies' room as if we were sorority sisters playing Truth or Dare."

"We haven't exchanged any secrets yet," Sally said. "But I think it's time we started. Ellen can tell hers first."

Ellen rummaged through her purse and brought out a comb; then she ran it through her black hair. When she was finished, she put the comb back and closed the purse.

"All right," she said. "It was right under your nose all the time, but of course you never knew it. Neither did Fieldstone nor anyone else."

"You couldn't expect men to notice anything," Vera said. "Their powers of observation are quite limited, and even if they'd known, they would most likely have approved." She gave Sally another glance. "A woman should be more perceptive, though."

"More perceptive of what?" Sally asked. She was getting a little tired of being condescended to, and her irritation showed in her voice.

"At seeing what was going on. It should have been obvious to anyone."

"It wasn't obvious to me," Sally said.

"How true," Ellen said. "But then hardly anything is."

Sally remembered that when she was in high school, two of her classmates had gotten into a fight in the restroom. It had probably been about a boy, but Sally didn't really remember. At the time, she'd thought it was the stupidest thing that had ever happened. She couldn't understand why any girl would want to fight another girl, pull her hair, and try to gouge her eyes out. But now she was beginning to understand.

"I suppose we should stop teasing you," Vera said.

Ellen glared at her. "I'm not teasing," she said.

Vera smiled. "Of course not. But Dr. Good is getting a bit

irritated with our behavior, and I can't say that I blame her much."

"Humpf," Ellen said, and turned to inspect her face in the mirror.

Sally noted with regrettable satisfaction that Ellen's skin was blotchy and her lips were chapped.

Vera wasn't watching Ellen. Her attention was now all on Sally.

Vera said, "The sad truth about Val is that he liked younger women."

Sally couldn't help looking at Ellen, who didn't qualify as young by anyone's standards.

"I know what you're thinking," Vera said. "Ellen's a little older than Val."

Sally resisted the temptation to say that she had been thinking that Ellen was *lot* older than Val.

"You see," Vera went on, "Val didn't really care much about any of the women he dated. We were just a distraction. He actually preferred his students."

Sally tried not to let her mouth drop open. She didn't quite succeed. So that's what Ellen had been trying to tell her.

"Oh, don't be so surprised," Vera said. "Men are swine. You should know that by now. Once a woman reaches a certain age, they don't have any more interest in her."

Sally didn't think that was true of all men. She certainly *hoped* it wasn't, being of a certain age herself.

"Are you telling me that Val was fooling around with students?"

"That's one way of putting it," Vera said. "He got away with it because he was very, very careful."

"But you knew about it. Ellen knew about it. Why didn't you tell anyone?"

Vera looked thoughtful. "Good question. I thought about it, but I decided that Val's personal relationships were his own business. As long as the students weren't in his classes, what was the harm? He wasn't promising them grades for sex or anything like that."

"But they were *students*," Sally said.

"True, but he wasn't interested in the really young ones. He never went out with anyone who wasn't at least twenty-one."

Sally shook her head in disbelief. "I can't understand how he got away with it."

"It was easy," Vera said. "He was never seen with students outside of class. If he took them anywhere, it was well away from the campus, off on the other side of Houston. And the relationships always were purely platonic."

"I don't believe it," Sally said, though she really wasn't surprised.

"Believe it," Ellen said.

Vera nodded. "It's true. Val wasn't interested in sex. I should know. I tried to pique his interest more than once. I can't speak for Ellen."

Ellen apparently didn't want to speak for Ellen either. She looked in the mirror with her lips drawn in a tight line. Her silence told Sally all she needed to know.

"So he was dating students but not doing anything sexual with them?"

"That's right," Vera said.

"But Fieldstone is death on that sort of thing." Sally regretted her choice of the word *death*, but it was too late to change it. "Dating students is strictly against the school's code of conduct. Fieldstone would have fired Val in a heartbeat if he'd known, and the Board would have backed him all the way."

"That's why Val kept it undercover," Vera said. "And it's also why he never did anything sexual, unless you count looking."

"Looking?"

"He liked to paint them," Vera said.

"Tammi Thompson," Sally said. "He was painting her."

"Yes. But I don't think he touched her, not in any sexual way."

"He told you about that?"

"Val and I were friends. We didn't have any secrets between us."

Ellen remained silent. Sally wasn't sure whether she knew about the incident with Tammi or not.

"Do you think that the rest of Val's story was true?" Sally asked.

"The rest?"

"That Tammi had asked him to do the painting for her husband."

"Of course not. She was letting him paint her because he asked her to. I told you that he liked to look."

"Then he lied to me," Sally said, though she was hardly shocked.

"And it wasn't the first time," Vera said, smiling wickedly. "Ain't that just like a man?"

Jorge and Jack were waiting in the church parking lot. The casket had been loaded into the hearse, which had pulled away several minutes before. Those going to the cemetery had followed the hearse, and most of the cars and people were gone.

Jack and Jorge were standing beside Jorge's black Celica. Jorge was smoking a Marlboro. He had apologized to Jack for lighting up, explaining that he had gotten into the habit in prison and had never been able to break it.

"I don't mind," Jack said. He didn't want to pry into Jorge's prison experiences. He was afraid of what he might find out. "I wonder if Ellen's all right."

Jorge blew a thin line of smoke from each nostril, and then flicked ashes from the tip of the Marlboro.

"I'm sure she's fine. The funeral was just too much for her. Women get emotional sometimes."

"So do men," Jack said.

Jorge contemplated the end of his cigarette, then dropped it to the ground and stepped on it.

"I know," he said.

Jack wished he'd kept his mouth shut. Considering the stories he'd heard about Jorge, he was pretty sure that Jorge knew a lot more about losing control of his emotions than Jack did.

He was saved from having to say anything more when he looked up and saw Sally coming out of the church. Ellen and Vera were right behind her. Vera had an arm around Ellen's shoulders as if supporting her.

Jorge started toward them. Vera met him and said a few words that Jack couldn't hear, and all of them started toward Jorge's car.

"Ellen's fine," Jorge told Jack. "We won't be going to the cemetery."

He unlocked the Celica, and Vera climbed into the back-seat, revealing quite a bit of leg in the process. But not so much that Jack didn't notice that she had to shove something aside in order to have room for herself.

He felt Sally stiffen beside him. He turned to say something, but she grabbed his left arm and squeezed. Taking this as a sign to keep his mouth shut, he said nothing as Jorge helped Ellen into the front seat.

"I'll see you at the college tomorrow," Jorge said. "Maybe things will be getting back to normal by then."

"Sure," Jack said.

Sally didn't say anything. She stood there gripping Jack's arm until Jorge had driven away.

When the Celica reached the street, she asked, "What was that in the backseat?"

"I'm not sure," Jack said. "It might have been a painting of some kind."

Sally relaxed her grip. "I was afraid that's what you were going to say."

30

After they left the church, Sally met Jack at Bumblebee's, a coffee shop not far from the college. It was really just an old house that had been remodeled, and at that time in the afternoon it was practically empty. Sally and Jack had their own private dining room, which had once been a bedroom.

Sally ordered some kind of flavored coffee. Jack, who didn't like coffee of any kind, no matter what the flavor, asked for a Diet Pepsi. He didn't like Diet Pepsi, either, but he felt that he should buy something if he was going to sit in the coffee shop and take up space.

When the drinks had been served, he said, "Now what's this about a painting?"

Sally told him the story, only some of which he'd heard before.

"So I think the painting is significant," she finished. "But I don't know what to do about its being in Jorge's car."

"Maybe I didn't see a painting," Jack said. "There was a blanket over it. Maybe it was something else."

"The blanket slipped when Vera moved it. It was a painting, all right. It was *the* painting."

"You're sure?

"I'm sure."

She wasn't really sure, but she couldn't imagine what other painting Jorge would have in the backseat of his car. It had to be the one of the goat.

"So what's Jorge doing with it?" Jack asked.

"That's what I'd like to know."

Jack took a sip of his Diet Pepsi and made a face. Maybe he should have gotten coffee after all.

"Can't you just ask him?"

Sally laughed. Jack thought she had a nice laugh. He wondered what he could do to make her laugh again.

So he said, "Maybe I could ask him."

Sally didn't laugh. "I don't think that would be a good idea. I'm sure that missing painting has something to do with Val's murder. If we ask Jorge, he'll know that we're onto him. And that wouldn't be good."

Jack thought about it. "I guess my idea about the murder's not any good then, either."

"Oh," Sally said. "I'm sorry, Jack. I'd forgotten that you had something to tell me. I just rushed into my own story without even asking."

"That's okay. I was probably wrong in what I was thinking, anyway."

"Maybe not. Go ahead. Tell me."

Jack looked at his Diet Pepsi. All the ice had melted, and the drink was an unappetizing yellowish color. He didn't think he'd have any more of it.

"Well," he said, "I had the idea that maybe Tammi killed Val. Say she went to his office and confronted him. Maybe he said something that set her off. Sometimes people get enraged and act out of the emotion of the moment. She could have grabbed the first thing that came to hand and hit him with it."

Sally nodded, remembering what Weems had said in Val's office.

"The police said that it might have been a crime of opportunity."

Jack was encouraged. If the police were thinking along the same lines, he might be onto something.

"After that, she could have panicked. She probably would have gone back to the store and told her husband what she'd done. Then he panicked, or lost his temper, and it happened all over again. Except that this time, *he* was the one who grabbed something."

"It could have happened," Sally said.

Jack smiled. He was feeling better about his idea. Move over, Sherlock Holmes.

"But it just doesn't fit," Sally said.

Jack's smile disappeared. "Why not? Because of the painting?"

"That's only part of it. The other part is what Ellen and Vera told me in the restroom."

She told Jack what she'd discovered about Val's relationships.

"Sounds like Tammi's husband has the best motive, then," Jack said.

Sally nodded. "That's what the police think, and they don't even know the whole story."

"But you don't agree."

"No. There are too many problems with that theory."

"The painting again."

"That's right. I still don't see how the painting fits in, but it disappeared at the same time Val was killed, so there has to be a connection. And then there's Ellen."

"Ellen? What does she have to do with all this?"

"She was involved with Val for a while. And I saw a list of the guests at the art show. She was in the gallery shortly before he was killed."

"So it could have been a . . . what did you call it?"

"Crime of opportunity?"

"That's it. Except that it wasn't Tammi Thompson who committed it. Ellen was in the art gallery, right near Val's office. She and Val talked and she got angry about his relationship with Tammi, lost her temper, grabbed the statue, and whacked him."

"It's possible," Sally said. "But that doesn't explain the missing painting. And there's more. Jorge was in the gallery that afternoon, too."

"Sounds like the art gallery was more crowded than the Galleria on Saturday afternoon."

Sally didn't laugh, but at least she smiled.

"That's right. And Coy Webster was around, too. He's been living there."

"You're kidding."

Sally told Jack about Coy's troubles.

"I never know what's going on around the school," Jack said. "I need to get out of the office more often."

"You and me both," Sally agreed.

"Is Coy in the clear on this?"

"He says he was out when Val was killed. Maybe he's telling the truth. The police think so. I think he knows something, though."

"But he's not talking."

"True."

"And Jorge has the painting."

"Yes. Which everyone tells me to forget about."

"So where does that leave us?" Jack asked.

Sally turned her nearly empty coffee cup in her hands.

"I don't know," she said.

Jack tried to think of something, but nothing came. He supposed Sherlock Holmes didn't have to worry about being shoved aside after all.

"Do you remember a movie called *Animal House*?" Sally asked.

The phrase that leapt to Jack's mind was *non sequitur*, but he didn't say that. He said, "Sure I remember it. It was the story of my freshman year in college."

Sally smiled. "Were you Otter?"

"That would be me."

"Good. I was afraid you might have been Bluto. But he's the one I was thinking of. I think he's the one we need to consider as a role model right now."

"Why?"

"Do you remember the scene where someone says that the situation calls for some kind of action, something really stupid?"

"Yeah. And Bluto says, 'And we're just the guys who can do it.'"

"That's the scene, all right."

"And you're thinking?"

"Of doing something really stupid."

"Well," Jack said, "we're just the guys who can do it."

31

————

Sally wasn't sure just when she'd decided to take Jack on as her partner in crime. Or anticrime. And she still wasn't sure what their relationship was. At any rate, Jack seemed like a nice guy, and since he'd been in on finding Tammi's body, maybe he deserved a chance to help her crack the case.

Crack the case, she thought. *I haven't done a thing, and I'm already starting to think in clichés from bad novels.*

Her plan was simple. They would take the painting from Jorge's car, bring it to Chief Desmond, and confront him with the fact that Jorge must have removed it from the art gallery.

"And then what?" Jack asked.

"Nothing. That's all we do. After that, we're out of it. Desmond can turn things over to Weems and the locals, and they'll figure out just how Jorge is involved."

"I have an idea about that," Jack said. "Jorge's involvement, I mean. Would you like to hear it?"

"Of course."

Jack looked around. There were people coming into the coffee shop now, and it wouldn't be long before there were

187

others seated in the room with them. The tables were too close together for confidential conversations, and besides, Jack wanted something stronger than a Diet Pepsi.

"Could I tell you about it at dinner?"

Sally had to think about that for a minute. She had never dated anyone from the school, and she wasn't sure she wanted to start, no matter how nice Jack seemed.

But it wouldn't actually be a date, she reminded herself. They were discussing a plan. And after dinner, they would be putting the plan into action.

So she said, "Only if you let me pay for myself."

"Sounds good to me," Jack said.

They wound up at the Old Mexico, a restaurant that had been in Hughes for as long as most people could remember. It had been opened by Emilio Parra shortly after the Second World War, and he had managed it for over forty years. When Emilio stepped down, his son Roberto took over.

Jack ordered a chili relleno, and Sally decided on the veggie enchiladas.

"And I'll have a Dos Equis," Jack told the waiter, one of Roberto's sons. "Sally?"

For just a second, Sally hesitated. What if someone from the college were to see the two of them sitting there drinking Mexican beer?

On the other hand, who cared?

"Sounds good to me," she said.

At Jack's request, they were seated in a booth at the back of the restaurant, not exactly secluded, but not within easy hearing distance of anyone else who might come in.

The waiter came back with two frosty bottles of Dos Equis and two glasses. He poured the beer for the two of them and left the bottles on the table.

Jack took a sip of beer. It was a lot better than a Diet Pepsi.

"So," Sally said. "What's your idea about Jorge?"

"I've actually told you already," Jack confessed. "But it seems to make more sense now."

"You mean about Jorge and Vera going to Val's office to talk to Val and killing him there?"

It sounded weak, even to Jack. Just as it had the last time he'd mentioned it to Sally. But he kept on going.

"Jorge could have done it."

"You said that before, too. I didn't believe it then."

"I know," Jack said. "I guess I shouldn't have brought it up again."

"But it does make more sense now," Sally said.

Jack brightened. "It does?"

"Well, maybe not. But there's the painting."

"Right. It ties Jorge to the murder."

Sally drank some of her beer. "I wouldn't go that far, not if Vera is the killer."

"Why not?"

"Because the painting doesn't fit in with your idea that the murder has something to do with Vera, that's why. Vera doesn't have any connection to the painting."

"As far as we know, she doesn't," Jack said. "But what if there's something we *don't* know?"

"There's not," Sally said. "Not about Vera, at least. I almost wish there were."

"Maybe we could think of something."

"No. The painting's connected with the prison, not with Vera."

"The prison," Jack said. "Ah-ha."

"Ah-ha?"

"Sure. Who do we know who has served time in prison?"

"Jorge. But we already know he has something to do with the painting. He brought it to the school, and it's in his car right now."

"Unless he ditched it," Jack said, and then he had another idea. "What if he went to the gallery and got into some kind of argument with Val about the painting?"

Sally thought about it. She could imagine Jorge swelling with anger, his muscles cording under his shirt as he split the back out of his suit. She wondered why she kept having fantasies about Jorge. It didn't seem very healthy. She shook her head.

"Why would he have killed Val?" she asked. "And why take the painting?"

"We could always ask him."

Sally didn't laugh this time. "I just don't think that would be a good idea. We can't let him know we suspect him. If he thinks we're onto him, he'll just get rid of the painting."

"Well, we can't let that happen," Jack said. "After all, we're going to do something really stupid about the painting."

Sally was about to agree, but the food arrived on sizzling hot plates. They stopped talking about the painting and began to eat.

When they were done and the waiter had brought the check, Jack said, "Are you sure you want to pay for yours?"

"Yes," Sally said, without hesitation.

Jack looked at the check. "Then you owe seven dollars and twenty-nine cents. Plus a tip."

Sally opened her purse and got out the money.

It was dark when they left the restaurant, but that didn't mean the college parking lot would be dark. It was always well-lighted. Sally wasn't worried about being seen, however. She wasn't planning to be there long.

"You're sure Jorge is working tonight?" Jack asked on the way.

"He works every night," Sally said. "That's why he can

come in so late every morning. He told me once that he likes it that way."

Someone had to be on campus in the evenings to help with the copy machine, to take phone calls from part-time instructors who might be coming in late or not at all, and to handle any minor emergencies that might crop up.

The campus police didn't want the job. They had plenty of other things to do.

None of the administrators or department chairs wanted the job, either. They wanted to spend their evenings at home unless they were teaching.

But Jorge liked the work, and after being at the college for only one semester, he had volunteered for it. No one tried to talk him out of it.

Sally drove the Acura into the parking lot. They had left Jack's car at the restaurant.

"Do you know where Jorge usually parks?" Jack asked.

"No," Sally said. "But the most convenient faculty spots are down by the Art and Music Building."

"Convenient?" Jack said.

"Yes. And it would be convenient for anyone taking a painting out of the building, too."

Jack spotted the Celica. It was in a faculty spot, all right, but it was surrounded by cars with student stickers. The police patrolled the lot in the evening, but they never ticketed anyone.

"What if the cops catch us?" he asked.

"We'll just have to be quick," Sally said, "and get our business taken care of before they come around to this part of the lot again."

She pulled into a spot that was as close to the Celica as she could get.

"Now comes the hard part," she said.

Jack knew what she meant. It had sounded possible when

she'd told him about it at the coffee shop. Stupid, yes, but possible.

Now it just sounded stupid, but he knew he had to go through with it. He didn't want Sally to think he was a coward.

They got out of the car, their faces eerie in the yellowish parking-lot lights. Sally opened the Acura's trunk. Lying inside it was something called a slim jim, a long thin piece of metal that the campus police used to open locked car doors.

"I locked my keys in the car a week ago," Sally had explained to Jack. "Desmond couldn't send anyone to help me, and he was busy, too, so he just gave me the slim jim and told me to open the car myself."

"He's a trusting soul."

"He didn't trust me at all. He was just too rushed to be any help, and I was pretty upset. So he got rid of me the best way he could."

Jack looked at the slim jim. "So you know how to use that thing?"

"It took me awhile, but I finally got the door unlocked. You just slide the slim jim down beside the window glass, and if you get it in the right place, you can pop the lock."

"Desmond didn't want his slim jim back?"

"I'm sure he did. I just forgot about it. I can give it back to him when we present him with the painting."

Looking down at the slim jim now, Jack wondered what he was doing there. He wasn't the criminal type, and his palms were getting sweaty. But he reached down and got the slim jim anyway. When he did, he saw the pistol case.

"What's this?" he asked.

Sally told him. "I was hoping to get in some target practice today. I didn't think about the funeral."

"You take target practice?"

"Now and then. It relaxes me."

192

Jack was beginning to wonder about Sally. She shot pistols, and she knew how to jimmy a car door. He wasn't the criminal type, but maybe she was.

He pushed the trunk shut and looked around the parking lot. There was no one around. The students and instructors were all safely inside, in the classrooms.

"The coast is clear," Jack said.

"Now *you're* doing it," Sally said.

"Doing what?"

"Never mind. Let's go."

They started toward Jorge's car. Jack had a sudden thought.

"What if the doors aren't locked?"

"They'll be locked. He wouldn't leave the painting in the car without locking the doors."

"Makes sense."

They were at the car then, and Jack tried the door handle. It was locked, all right. He looked inside.

"There's another possibility," he said, turning to Sally.

"What's that?"

"Have a look," Jack said.

Sally glanced into the car's interior. The painting wasn't there.

32

N ow what?" Jack said, secretly relieved that he wasn't going to have to engage in any overtly criminal activity.

"Maybe he put it in the trunk," Sally said.

A cold sweat popped out on Jack's forehead. Trying to open the car door was one thing. Trying to open the trunk was something else. He was sure that even Sally had never done anything like this before.

Or had she?

"I don't think it would be a good idea to break into the trunk," Jack said. "Especially since that's the patrol car coming around the corner."

Sally saw the white police car moving slowly in their direction. She held the slim jim at her side, making it nearly invisible.

"Let's put this thing back in my car," she said. "I have a feeling I know where the painting is."

"Where?" Jack asked, holding his breath as the patrol car passed slowly by the end of the row where they were standing.

"You'll see," Sally said, without even a glance in the car's direction. "I don't think he got rid of it, though."

Sally opened the trunk and returned the slim jim to its place. Jack pushed the trunk shut again.

"All right," he said. "Now, where's the painting?"

"Follow me," Sally said, and headed in the direction of the art gallery.

They climbed the stairs to the gallery and looked through the glass doors. There was a light on in the gallery, and high on the wall there was a TV camera moving slowly from side to side. Desmond had already installed the security system, though it didn't make Sally feel any safer.

The painting of the goat was hanging on the wall at the end of the gallery as if it had never been gone.

"Are you sure it wasn't there all along?" Jack asked when Sally pointed it out.

Sally gave him a look that made him wish he'd kept his mouth shut.

"There's something different about that goat," she said. "I have to get a closer look."

She tried the door handle, and the door swung open.

"Why isn't the door locked?" Jack asked.

"They never lock the rooms until after classes are over," Sally said. "There might be a class in here some evening, so the doors are left open."

"No wonder things get stolen. It would have been easy for Jorge to replace the painting any time he wanted to."

"Yes. Now let's have a look at it."

They walked to the end of the gallery. The painting didn't look any different to Jack, but then he hadn't studied it very carefully in the first place.

Sally had. "It's not the same. The 666 is gone."

"I thought you told me it was never there."

"It wasn't. But Roy Don Talon thought it was, which was the important thing. In fact, I thought he was the one who'd taken the painting. If we hadn't seen it in Jorge's car, I would have confronted Talon about it."

"That might not have been a good idea."

"I'm not afraid of Roy Don Talon. But someone obviously is. This painting's been altered. You can see what that means."

Jack wasn't sure that he could. He'd already had so many theories shot down that he didn't even want to venture a guess this time.

"I'm afraid I can't see a thing," he said.

"It means that Naylor and Fieldstone didn't trust the judgment of an independent panel. That was just something they cooked up. I thought it was Talon who didn't trust a panel to make the right decision, but I had it backward."

Jack thought he had it now. "So that's why no one wanted to talk about the missing painting. They knew that Jorge was altering it. Now they can call in their panel, and everyone will see something that looks like the head of an ordinary goat."

"That's right, except that I don't think Jorge made the alterations. I think he took the painting to the prisoner who created it. That way, the same paint could be used. The change is subtle, but it's enough to make sure that there's no sign of a 666 anywhere, not even if you're looking for it. After the panel examines the painting and finds nothing suspicious, Naylor and Fieldstone will bring Talon back, and if he says anything, they'll just claim that his eyes were playing tricks on him when he thought he saw the 666. It might even work."

Jack should have been outraged at the deceit being practiced by the college's administrators, but he wasn't. For one thing, they had defended the painting to begin with and stood up against censorship. So what if they were cheating a little? It was for a good cause, and he didn't really blame them. So what he felt instead of outrage was relief.

"That means that Jorge's in the clear," he said. "He didn't kill Val."

"I wouldn't be so sure of that," Sally said. "Val would have argued against anything as dishonest as switching the paintings, as well he should have. He might have been a philanderer, but he had high principles when it came to art. He wouldn't have wanted to cheat. He didn't think there was anything wrong with the painting as it was, and he wouldn't have budged from that opinion."

Jack felt a little guilty for siding with the administration, but he didn't mention it.

He said, "And you don't think Jorge could have persuaded him to change his mind?"

"No way."

"So he killed him?"

"I'm not saying that, but it looks suspicious."

"Fieldstone and Naylor may bend the rules their way now and then," Jack said. "But I don't think they'd cover for a murderer."

"Not if they knew they were doing it. It wouldn't just get them in trouble; it would cause too much bad publicity for the school. But surely you don't think Jorge would have told them if he'd killed Val."

"No," Jack said. "Now that you mention it, I don't suppose he would have. It seems like the sort of thing he'd want to keep quiet."

Jack looked glumly at the painting. There was no way he and Sally could prove that it had ever been gone, especially if Naylor and Fieldstone backed Jorge.

"So what do we do now?" Jack asked.

"I don't have any idea," Sally said. "Go home, I guess."

Jack heard a noise behind them. He turned to see what had made it, but there was no one there. Except for Sally and him, the gallery was deserted.

"The classrooms," Sally said.

"What do you think it was?"

"Probably nothing. But we should look."

Jack didn't want to look. Not that he was afraid. He just didn't think it was important. But Sally did, so he would have to look.

He went toward the classroom. The door was closed, and it was dark inside.

"Maybe someone's showing a video to a class in there," he said, not believing a word of it.

"There aren't any classes in here this evening," Sally said. "If there were, we would have heard something earlier."

Jack put his hand on the door handle just as the door was flung open.

He tried to jump back, but he tripped over his own foot and the door hit him in the face. He was stunned, and went down backward. He tried to catch himself, but he wasn't successful. His arms collapsed under him, and his head bounced off the unpadded Berber carpet.

He shook his head and started to sit up, but a dark shape barreled out of the door and planted a foot squarely in the middle of his stomach.

"Oooooofffff!" Jack said as all the air gushed out of his lungs and he fell back limply on the floor.

33

S ally didn't wait around to see if Jack was all right. Instead, she took off after Coy Webster, who, after stepping on Jack's stomach, had scooted out the gallery door with his baggy pants flapping around his legs.

By the time Sally got outside, Coy was already in the parking lot. *He must have taken the stairs three at a time,* Sally thought. She couldn't imagine how he'd done it, not in those pants.

She didn't know what kind of car Coy drove, but there was an ancient gray Dodge Dart in the lot, right under one of the light towers. Sally wasn't surprised when Coy headed straight for the Dart.

"Coy!" she called. "Wait a minute!"

Coy either didn't hear her or didn't want to wait, so she hurled herself down the stairs as fast as she dared. Coy was inside the Dart by the time she got to the lot.

Luckily, he was having a bit of difficulty getting the car started. Every time he turned the key, the starter ground noisily and the Dart shuddered like a palsied dog.

When Sally reached the car, Coy still hadn't gotten it started. He was sitting behind the wheel with a look of intense concentration, the starter grinding away, the car jittering up and down and from side to side.

Sally tapped on the closed window. Coy looked up, startled, and then turned back and tried to start the car again.

"It's not going to start," Sally yelled. "Give it a rest, Coy. I just want to talk to you."

Coy gave it one more try. This time, there was much less grinding. The battery was about to give up. Coy turned off the ignition and slumped back against the car seat, a look of frustration on his face.

Sally tapped on the window again. Coy didn't move for a second or two. Then he sat up a little straighter and rolled the window down.

"Why don't we go back inside?" Sally said. "We could talk for a minute, and we could see about Jack."

"Jack Neville?" Coy said. "Is he the one I ran over?"

"I'm sure he won't hold it against you," Sally said, though she wasn't sure at all.

"It was an accident," Coy said. "I didn't intend to hurt him. He frightened me."

"I'm sure you didn't intend to hurt anyone. What were you afraid of?"

"I was afraid you'd tell Chief Desmond that I was sleeping in the classroom tonight. He told me not to let it happen again, but I didn't have anywhere else to go. I don't even have a class on another campus tonight."

"I won't say anything to Desmond," Sally assured him. "Let's go see about Jack."

Coy got out of the car with considerable reluctance and stood beside it. His skin looked like greenish pastry in the parking-lot light.

"Don't worry about Jack," Sally said. "He won't hurt you."

"That's easy for you to say. You didn't run over him."

"He'll be fine," Sally said, and as if to confirm her statement, Jack appeared at the foot of the stairs.

"See?" Sally said.

Jack shuffled toward them, listing slightly to his right. He had his right arm wrapped around his stomach.

"He doesn't look fine to me," Coy said, looking as if he might make a dive for the Dart's interior.

Jack didn't look fine to Sally, either. She said, "Maybe we could just talk right here."

"What about?" Coy asked.

Sally didn't have a chance to answer because Jack had reached them.

"Is this who stepped on me?" he asked.

"It was an accident," Coy said. "I was in a hurry, and I didn't see you."

"You stepped on me."

"I apologize. I really didn't intend to. I guess I panicked."

"What I'd like to know is why you panicked," Sally said. "After all, you know both of us. We don't pose much of a threat."

Coy tugged at his too-large shirt. "I told you. I was afraid you'd tell Desmond about me."

"That's not good enough," Sally said. "You were too scared for that to be it. You heard us talking, didn't you?"

Coy turned toward his Dart again, as if wishing he were inside it and driving along a freeway in upstate New York.

"You know something about that painting," Sally said. "And it's time you told someone about it."

"Someone like us," Jack said. He was still holding his stomach, still listing a little, and his breathing was slightly ragged.

"I don't want to get anyone in trouble," Coy said.

"Don't worry about that," Sally said. "We won't repeat anything you tell us."

"Are you sure?"

"Of course," Sally said. "Jack?"

Jack didn't look nearly as certain as Sally sounded, but he said, "Oh, all right."

The patrol car that they had seen earlier came around the corner again, moving slowly along.

"Why don't we go back inside?" Sally said.

"Good idea." Jack turned and started toward the art gallery.

Coy didn't say anything, but he followed Jack. Sally trailed along behind. She smiled and waved cheerily at the patrol car.

Nothing wrong here, Officer. Just three happy instructors out for a pleasant evening stroll.

And Sally had to admit that it was a lovely evening. There was a soft breeze, the air was mild, and the humidity wasn't as high as usual, which meant that your skin didn't scum over with greasy moisture within ten seconds of leaving an air-conditioned building.

Unfortunately, the situation Sally found herself in wasn't as pleasant as the weather. She wasn't even sure she wanted to hear the answers that Coy would give her. But like most teachers, she had an intense curiosity, and she was certainly going to ask the questions.

They entered the art gallery and went directly to the classroom. Jack flipped on the lights, and Sally went to the front row of desks.

"We can sit here," she said.

Coy went over and sat beside her. Jack pulled the chair from the teacher's desk over in front of them.

"Now," Sally said to Coy, "I want to know exactly what you saw and heard on the day Val Hurley was killed."

34

Coy looked around the room. Sally followed his gaze and saw the green duffel bag in the corner. She supposed that it contained all Coy's worldly belongings.

"Coy?" she said.

Coy turned to look at her. "I didn't see Val get killed or anything like that. I was in here all the time, right up until I left the campus. I never went in Val's office. I don't even know if he was killed while I was here."

"Could it have happened then?" Jack asked.

"I guess so. I can't hear very well in here with the door closed."

"You heard us," Sally pointed out.

"But you were in the gallery. Val would have been in his office. If he was there. And I'm not saying he was."

"A. B. D. wasn't in the gallery. He was in Val's office, and you heard him, all right."

Coy shook his head. "I wish I'd never mentioned that. Troy Beauchamp has a way of worming things out of you."

"But you did mention it," Sally said.

205

"I know. That was different, too. A. B. D. and Val were yelling so loudly that I couldn't help hearing."

"But yelling is all you heard?"

"That's right. You heard what I told Chief Desmond. As far as I know, there was no fighting, no scuffling, nothing. After the shouting was over, A. B. D. must have left quietly."

"You didn't check to see if Val was okay?" Jack asked.

"No. There wasn't any fighting, just yelling."

"As far as you know," Jack said.

"That's right. As far as I know."

"Was that before or after Jorge came in?"

"That was before."

"So it's possible that Val didn't come out to stop Jorge because he was already dead."

"I guess so," Coy said. "But it's also possible that he had his door closed and didn't see Jorge. He was pretty quiet, except for when he opened the door."

"Let's start over," Sally said. "Coy, when exactly were you here, in this room, on the day Val was killed?"

Coy ducked his head. "From around three o'clock until six."

"That's not what you told Desmond," Sally said.

"Oh. Well, I could be wrong. I'm not really sure when I left."

Coy looked at the ceiling and closed his eyes as if trying to visualize what he'd done that afternoon.

"Oh, wait, now I remember. I left early to get a hamburger, so I wasn't here much past four. Anyone could have come in after I left."

Jack thought that Coy would make a terrible witness when the case came to trial. If it ever did.

"You saw Jorge Rodriguez come in here, didn't you?" he asked.

Coy looked as if he might cry. "Yes," he said. "I saw him. But I don't want him to know that."

"Why not?" Sally asked.

"Because."

It was almost as if they were talking to a small child, Jack thought. He had to resist the temptation to say, "Because why?"

Sally said, "If you didn't see him kill Val, and if you didn't hear Jorge kill Val, you shouldn't have anything to worry about."

"I've heard stories about Jorge," Coy said.

Jack wondered if the stories Coy had heard were the same ones that Jack had heard. He was about to ask, but something else occurred to him.

"Wait a minute," Jack said. "You keep telling us that you didn't see anything, but you saw Jorge take the painting. How did that happen?"

Coy opened his mouth, closed it, opened it again, closed it. He looked a little like a curious fish looking out through the glass of an aquarium.

Finally, he said, "Sometimes I hear the outside door open, and I glance out to see who's come in. I don't open the classroom door, though. I don't want anyone to know that I'm in here."

Jack looked over his shoulder. The classroom door had a small rectangular pane of glass set in the right-hand side.

Sally didn't look at the door. She said, "How long was Jorge in the gallery?"

Coy had to think about that. When he came up with the answer, he smiled a relieved smile.

"Not long at all. Not long enough for Val and him to have any kind of discussion. He must have taken the painting down and left right away."

"You didn't actually see him take it off the wall, then?"

"No, but I saw him when he went out. He was carrying a painting."

"Did anyone else come in during the afternoon?" Jack asked.

Coy nodded. "I'm sure there were others. I don't remember."

"What about Ms. Baldree?" Sally asked.

"Oh," Coy said. "She's the one with the really black hair, isn't she?"

"That's Ellen," Sally said. "Did you see her?"

Coy's answer was hesitant. "I think so."

"You either saw her or you didn't see her," Jack said. "Which is it?"

Coy hung his head. "All right. I saw her."

"And how long was she here?" Sally asked.

"I don't know."

"Don't start that again," Jack said.

"I mean it. I don't know. I was looking over a few essays that I'd graded, and I didn't see her leave."

"So she could have been here when you left," Jack said.

"That's right. Or she might have been gone. I wasn't listening for the door. I might not have heard her leave."

"We'll let that go for a minute," Sally said. "Who else came in?"

"No one." This time Coy sounded positive. But he wasn't. "Well, what I mean is that I didn't hear anyone or see anyone. That doesn't mean no one came in. But if anyone did, I didn't hear it. Or see it."

Once again, Jack thought about the kind of witness Coy would make. Jack would have hated to be one of the lawyers trying the case, especially whichever one Coy was testifying for.

"Anyway," Coy went on, "there's something else about Ms. Baldree. She came in before Mr. Rodriguez did."

Now that was interesting, Jack thought. "How long before?" he asked.

"Ten or fifteen minutes, I guess. I wasn't keeping track, you know. I didn't expect anyone to be killed."

"And you don't know when she left," Sally said.

"That's right."

Sally looked at Jack. He knew what she must have been thinking. Jorge didn't meet any opposition when he took the painting, so most likely Val hadn't known about it being taken. Was he closeted in his office with Ellen, or was he already dead?

Whichever was the case, they weren't going to find out from Coy. He either didn't know or wasn't going to tell them. Jack questioned him for another minute or two but got absolutely no other information from him.

"Isn't there anyone you can spend the nights with?" Sally asked Coy, changing the subject. "You know you can't continue to stay in this classroom."

"I don't see why not. I'm not hurting anyone."

"It's not safe here," Jack said. "What if the killer comes back?"

Coy blinked. "He wouldn't do that, would he? Why would he do that?"

"Killers always return to the scene of the crime," Jack said.

Sally raised her eyebrows at him.

"I was only kidding," Jack said, just as he heard the outside door open.

35

Sally never took her pistol out of the car except to carry it to the firing range. She'd never even thought about taking it anywhere else.

But for just a second, as the outside door of the art gallery hissed shut on its automatic closer, she wished that she'd brought the pistol with her and that she had it in her hand at that very instant.

There was nothing she could do about it now. The pistol was down in the parking lot, locked in the trunk of her Acura, where it was doing her no good at all.

She looked around the classroom. There was no place to hide except under the teacher's desk in front of the room, and Coy Webster had scrabbled across the floor like a spider and beaten her there. For a man with baggy pants, he could really move when he wanted to.

Jack had moved quickly as well. He was standing beside the classroom door, holding the straight chair that had been behind the teacher's desk.

As Sally watched, the door began to open, and Jack raised the chair over his head.

"Don't, Jack!" Sally yelled, as Tom Clancey poked his head through the door.

Jack had already begun to swing the chair downward, but Clancey, warned by Sally's cry, ducked back outside as it descended.

The chair passed through the space that he had vacated, and its back legs bounced off the floor.

Clancey, looking apprehensive, stood just outside the room and drew his revolver.

"All right!" he said. "What's going on in there?"

"Nothing, Sergeant Clancey," Sally said. "Mr. Neville and I were in here discussing something related to the art department, and you frightened us. We thought you were a prowler."

Clancey continued to stand outside the door, and he didn't holster his pistol.

"You're the prowlers, not me," he said. "Someone called the dispatcher and reported that there were lights on in the gallery. Chief Desmond left specific instructions to check out anything suspicious in this building. He says there's been someone living in here."

"Well, it's not me," Jack said from beside the door, being careful not to step into the line of fire. "Dr. Good and I were just having a look around, checking to be sure that there was no one in this room. She's the division chair responsible for this department, you know."

"That's right," Sally said. "I thought it might be a good idea to make sure that Mr. Webster hadn't disobeyed Chief Desmond's order."

Clancey didn't appear to be convinced. "Well? *Did* he disobey the order?"

Jack stepped out from behind the door, leaving the chair

behind, and walked over to Sally. He waved a hand to indicate the empty room around them.

"You don't see him anywhere, do you?" he said.

Clancey stepped inside the room and looked around. If he noticed the duffel bag, he didn't seem to pay it any special attention. Maybe he thought it was just some piece of equipment related to the art classes. He put away his sidearm and relaxed slightly.

"No," he said. "I don't see him anywhere. But you two ought not to be here, either."

"I'm sorry if we caused you any trouble," Sally said.

"It's no trouble. You'll show up on the surveillance tapes, though."

Sally had forgotten about the newly installed camera. She wondered if Coy had known about it. Oh, well. He knew now.

"It would probably be a good idea if you two got out of here now," Clancey said. "I'll check around just to make sure there's no one else in the building."

"We'll be leaving in a few minutes," Sally said. "We have a few things to discuss first."

Clancey looked as if he wanted to ask what those things were, but he didn't.

"Okay, but be sure you turn off the lights when you leave. We don't want anyone else calling about prowlers."

"We'll take care of everything," Sally assured him.

"All right, then."

Clancey turned and left the room, but he didn't close the door. Sally was sure he'd left it open deliberately, so he could spy on them.

"I wonder what he really thinks we were doing in here," she said.

Jack was embarrassed. "I, uh, I—"

"Is he gone?" Coy Webster asked from under the desk.

"Stay there," Sally said.

213

Coy didn't come out, and he didn't ask any questions. He just stayed where he was.

"What about that camera?" Sally asked Jack.

"What about it?"

"How are we going to get Coy out of here without being taped?"

"I didn't know we were going to try."

"Well, we are. He can't stay here. He's sure to be caught, and there's no telling what Desmond might do. He might try to get him fired."

"Oh, no," Coy moaned. "He can't do that. I'd starve to death. I can't afford an apartment as it is. I'm already going to have to sleep in my car."

Sally thought that was an exaggeration. After all, Coy did have jobs on several other campuses. But he did need a place to stay.

"He can't sleep in his car," she said to Jack. "And it wouldn't look right if I let him stay at my place. What can we do?"

Jack sighed. "I know where you're going with this. You're not fooling anybody."

Sally looked as innocent as she could. "I don't know what you mean."

"Yes you do. But it's okay. I feel the same way, I guess. So Coy can stay with me, but only for tonight. Tomorrow, we're going to find him a place of his own. There's bound to be some low-rent apartment in town, maybe above a garage or something like that."

"You're sweet," Sally said.

"You really are," Coy said from under the desk.

Jack didn't have a chance to respond to either of them because Sergeant Clancey stuck his head in the door and said, "All clear. I'll be leaving now."

"We'll be gone in a minute," Sally said. "And we won't forget the lights."

"Thanks," Clancey said.

When Sally was sure that Clancey was out of the building, she told Coy Webster that he could come out.

He emerged from beneath the desk and apologized for deserting them and hiding.

"It was just a reflex. After what Chief Desmond said to me, I really didn't want him to catch me in here."

"Don't worry about it," Sally said. "We've got to get you out of here before someone else comes barging in."

Coy went to get his duffel bag, picking it up by the two thick nylon handles and hefting it to his side.

"It's great of you to take me in, Jack," he said. "I really appreciate it."

"It's only for tonight. After that, you're on your own."

Coy didn't say anything.

"And you can't come back here," Sally told him. "Now let's go."

"What about the video camera?" Jack asked.

"In the movies, someone usually sprays the lens with hair spray," Coy said.

Sally held up her purse. "No hair spray in here. I don't carry it. It never seems to help much."

"I think your hair looks fine," Jack said.

She smiled. "Thanks. Anyway, I don't think we have to worry about the camera. I bet they'll never check the tape unless something happens. Like another murder."

"You're probably right," Jack said. "If you're willing to chance it, I am."

"It doesn't bother me in the least. What about you, Coy?"

Coy said that he'd prefer not to be on tape. "They installed that camera this afternoon, after I was already in here, so they missed me then. But now I guess I don't have any choice."

"Maybe you do," Jack said. "Maybe we can do something about it. When we get to the gallery, you two keep right on going, no matter what I do. Got that?"

Sally and Coy nodded, and Jack led the way out of the room. Sally and Coy followed along behind. When Jack got into the gallery, he turned to the camera, did a little jig, tried a Michael Jackson moonwalk that didn't work so well, and took a deep bow. Then he went outside, where Sally and Coy were waiting.

"What was that all about?" Sally wanted to know.

"I figured that if anyone watches those tapes, he'll be so fascinated by my performance that he won't notice you two slinking out in the background."

"Fat chance," Sally said.

36

Coy's old Dart still wouldn't start, so Sally told him to leave it on the lot. Maybe the police would see it and think Coy was still around. Then they'd spend all night looking in the various buildings to see where Coy could be hiding. The exercise would do them good.

"You can ride with me and Jack," she said.

"Are you sure I won't be . . . interfering with anything?" he asked.

"I'm sure," Sally told him.

Coy tossed his duffel in the back of the Acura and tried to follow it. It required the sinuosity of an anaconda to twist around the front seat, but he finally managed to fit himself into the rear.

Jack got into the front and slid the seat back. Coy yelped when it slammed into his knees.

"Sorry," Jack said, easing forward an inch or so.

Sally got behind the wheel with a grace that put Jack and Coy to shame. She started the car and ejected the Bobby Vee

CD. Then she pulled out of the parking space.

"Speaking of finding Coy a place to stay," Jack said, "what do you think happened to Ralph Thompson? Why haven't the police been able to find him?"

"They're not looking in the right place," Sally said.

"Where would the right place be?"

Sally shrugged. "I have no idea."

"People on the run always go home," Coy said from the backseat.

Jack turned to look at him. "How do you know?"

"I teach in the prisons," Coy said, "so I know about fugitives. That's why they always get caught when they escape or violate their parole. They can't stay away from familiar places and familiar faces."

"Well, you can bet that Ralph Thompson's not at home," Sally said. "I'm sure Detective Weems has the place staked out."

"I didn't mean that he'd go home, necessarily," Coy said. "He might have gone to his parents' house. Or to a friend's place. Or even to his in-laws' home if there's a chance they don't think he murdered their daughter."

"I don't think he'd go to his in-laws' house," Jack said.

"Probably not," Coy said. "My in-laws don't like me at all, and I've never even killed anyone."

"We still don't know that Ralph killed anyone," Sally reminded them.

She'd been thinking about that ever since getting in the car. It seemed likely now that Jorge was innocent, and she was glad of that.

But there was always Ellen.

Not to mention A. B. D. Sally still wasn't convinced that he hadn't gone into a rage and killed Val. Coy might not have heard anything happen, but that didn't mean it hadn't been that way.

And if not A. B. D., what about others who might have been in the gallery after Coy had left? What about Vera?

For that matter, Sally wasn't entirely convinced of Coy's own innocence. Wasn't it possible that Val had objected to Coy's sleeping in the classroom? There could have been an argument, and Coy could have been the one who grabbed the little statue from the desk.

Maybe having him spend the night at Jack's house wasn't such a good idea after all. What if he got mad at Jack?

Sally shook her head. That was a ridiculous idea. Coy wasn't capable of killing anyone. He wasn't even capable of taking care of himself.

And of course, it was probably true that Ralph Thompson was the guilty party. All the signs pointed to it. She had been misled by the missing painting, but now that she had an idea why it had been taken, she could pretty much rule out its having anything to do with the murder.

She became aware that Coy was saying something to her.

"I'm sorry, Coy," she said. "I was drifting. Can you go over that again?"

"I was just saying that when people hide, they go somewhere that they feel safe. That's the important thing. It doesn't have to be a house or a place with someone they know, like in-laws or parents or friends. It could be a neighborhood or even a place of business. I had a student once who escaped and spent two nights hiding out in back of the Dairy Queen where he'd worked when he was a teenager. He ate out of the Dumpster and slept in a big cardboard box."

"I guess we could check out the Dairy Queen," Jack said. "Or maybe . . ."

His voice trailed off, and he looked at Sally, who knew exactly what he was thinking. She wished she didn't, but she did, no question.

"There was no one at the craft shop when we found Tammi's body," she said.

"I heard about that," Coy said. "It must have been terrible. I don't think I could have been as calm about it as you two."

Jack ignored him. "There wasn't anyone there *then*. But think about it. If Ralph Thompson listens to the radio at all, and you can bet he does, he knows the body's been found and removed. And speaking of bets, I'll make you one: I'll bet the police don't have a guard on the place. They won't expect him to come back there. His house, maybe, but not the shop. They probably won't even think of it."

"Edgar Allan Poe," Sally said.

"Huh?"

" 'The Purloined Letter.' To beat a criminal at his own game, you have to think like him. The police can't do it when the criminal is either much more stupid than they are, or a lot smarter."

"In this case, I hope you're thinking he's a lot smarter," Jack said. "Besides, I didn't come up with the idea. It was Coy."

"It doesn't matter whose idea it was. And I'm not even sure Ralph Thompson's guilty, much less whether you or Coy is smarter than the police. Besides, smart might not even enter into this. The Hughes Police don't have enough personnel to stake out too many places. I'm sure there won't be anyone at the store."

"Anyhow," Coy said from behind them, "what difference does it make? We're not going to do anything stupid like going to the Thompsons' craft shop."

Jack and Sally didn't answer.

Coy said, "Well, we aren't, are we?"

"Who, us?" Sally said. "We're professional educators, not

cops. So we're surely not going to do anything as stupid as driving by the craft shop, are we?"

She looked at Jack.

"I have a feeling that we are," he said.

37

———

Sally didn't really think that Ralph Thompson was hiding at his own shop. She wouldn't have driven by there if she had. She would have called Detective Weems and told him to check the place out.

Or that's what she told herself at first.

Then she thought about what Weems would say. He'd probably be condescending and tell her to leave investigating crime to the police. That's what Desmond had said, and the local police didn't seem to have a much higher opinion of her intelligence than Desmond did. In fact, they probably thought less of her than Desmond did, if that was possible.

Which meant that even if she called Weems, he wouldn't do anything. Or maybe he would. Maybe she had entirely mistaken his attitude toward her.

But she didn't think so. She was pretty sure he thought she was a totally incompetent woman, or maybe that she was incompetent *because* she was a woman. That's the attitude that Desmond seemed to have. So she wasn't going to call anyone.

She would, however, drive by the shop just to satisfy her

curiosity and to let Jack test his theory. After all, what was the worst that could happen?

Well, maybe that was the wrong question to ask. The worst that could happen was that Thompson would be there, that he would have armed himself with an Uzi, or whatever kind of assault weapon he could get from the illegal arms dealers in the Houston area, and that he would mow them down in the street as they drove past his place of business.

Sally thought again about the pistol in the trunk of the Acura. Maybe she should just start carrying it in a shoulder holster. Or in her purse, not that there would be much room for it there. She didn't carry hair spray, but she carried just about everything else. Sometimes she thought half the world's supply of crumpled facial tissue was in her purse, though she wasn't quite sure how it had all gotten there.

It was dark on the street where the Thompsons' shop was located, not because there were no streetlights but because the street was overhung by the limbs of the large oak trees that grew in every nearby yard.

It wasn't so dark, however, that Sally couldn't see the shadowy figure lurking near the rear of the building. She slowed the Acura to a crawl. She lifted her right hand from the wheel and pointed.

"Do you see anything back there?" she asked Jack.

"I do," Coy said. "There's someone standing by the building."

"He's right," Jack said. "Do you have a cell phone?"

"Yes," Sally said. She pulled the Acura to the curb and parked. "It's in the car pocket. Why?"

"Because I'm going to dial 911."

"Wait," Sally said. "Let's check things out first."

"I don't want to check things out," Coy said, sounding as if he wished there were a nearby desk to hide under. "I don't think that's a good idea at all."

Evidently, neither did Jack, who was trying to open the glove compartment.

"It's locked," Sally said. "Anyway, I don't think there's a lot to worry about."

The dark figure started toward the car. Coy slid off the seat and somehow managed to fit himself into the tiny space between the front and back seats.

Jack said, "Wait a minute. I know who that is."

"And it's not Ralph Thompson," Sally said. "It's that woman who was here when we found Tammi."

Jack rolled down his window. As the woman came closer, her orange hair seemed to glow in the dimness as if it might be radioactive. She was still wearing the orange pants that she'd had on the day before. Jack realized that he didn't know the woman's name.

"Hi," he said. "I'm Jack Neville. I met you here yesterday."

"I remember you," the woman said. "You're the one that found that poor girl's body."

"That's right. What are you doing back here?"

"I guess I could ask you the same question, now couldn't I?"

"You could, all right. We were just curious, that's all."

"I guess you didn't hear the dog barking, then, did you?"

"Dog?" Jack said. "What dog?"

"The one I told you about yesterday. The mean dog that Mr. Thompson keeps in his store."

"No," Jack said. "I didn't hear the dog."

Sally was tired of being left out of the conversation, so she got out of the car and walked around to stand by Jack's window.

"I'm Sally Good," she said. "I was here yesterday, too."

"Pleased to meet you," the woman said. "My name's Estelle Franks. Not too many people named Estelle around these days. Young people like different names now."

"I think Estelle's a very nice name," Sally said. "What about the dog?"

"I can hear things," Estelle said. "My daughter thinks I need a hearing aid, but I can hear just fine. I live two houses down the street, and I heard that dog, all right."

Sally and Jack didn't say anything. Coy was still huddled on the back floorboard, as if he were afraid that Estelle would suddenly turn into Tony Perkins, whip out a butcher knife, and slash them to death.

The night was very quiet. A slight breeze turned the leaves in the oaks, and an occasional car shushed by on a parallel street.

There was no dog barking.

"I know what you're thinking," Estelle said. "The dog's quiet now, but it wasn't quiet a few minutes ago. It was barking up a storm. I know what I heard. There was a light on in the back there, too."

There was no light on in the store now. The interior was quite dark, much darker even than the outside.

"I can see just as well as I can hear," Estelle said. "You needn't be thinking I can't see, because I can. I know a light when I see one."

"I'm sure you do," Sally said, looking at Jack, then back at Estelle. "How long did the dog bark?"

"Not long. I was watching *Dateline*, and I could hardly hear Jane Pauley for the barking. She's really cute, don't you think?"

Sally said she thought Jane Pauley was very nice.

"Well, she was doing that part about what year things happened in, and I couldn't hear her for the dog. But by the time I got over here, it had quit."

"You really shouldn't be coming over here alone," Sally said. "Mr. Thompson's a fugitive from justice."

She was sorry she'd said it as soon as the words left her mouth. She wondered what cliché she would come up with next.

"He doesn't scare me any, even if he is mean. I won't put up with a dog barking while I'm trying to watch TV."

Sally leaned down to the level of the Acura's window.

"What do you think?" she asked Jack.

"There could be someone in there, I guess."

"I think we should call the police," said Coy, who still hadn't moved from the floor.

Sally didn't think so. She was sure Weems would be worse than condescending when he heard about the dog and the light, no matter how credible Estelle sounded to Sally, who wasn't in any mood to be patronized. Even if Weems sent someone to search the building, it wouldn't be worth it. But if she had proof that someone was inside, Weems would have to be civil.

"Why don't you have a look?" she asked Jack.

Jack opened the car door and uncoiled himself from the seat. He stood up and walked over to the front window of the store.

"You can't see anything that way," Estelle said.

She was right. All Jack saw was his own dark reflection.

"You have go to the back, where the light was."

"There's no light now," Jack pointed out. "There aren't even any windows."

"The light was shining under that door," Estelle said. "The door you opened when you went inside."

"Oh," Jack said. "That door."

"Don't go messing around with any doors," Coy said. "Call the police."

"It wouldn't hurt to look," Sally said. "You don't have to go inside. But you do what you think is best."

Jack smiled and started toward the door. He didn't make

a sound as he strolled down the side of the building, not that he was trying to be especially quiet. Making noise might even be a good idea if someone was hiding in there, which Jack wasn't sure was the case.

And, like Sally, he wasn't a hundred percent convinced that Ralph Thompson was a murderer. Anyone might panic when faced with the prospect of being arrested. What if Thompson had found his wife dead and simply run away? Coy Webster would probably have done the same thing.

I might have done the same thing, Jack thought.

He went to the door and looked back at the car. Sally was standing beside it, talking to Estelle. There was no sign of Coy.

Jack rattled the door, a little more loudly than was necessary.

There was no answering sound from inside the shop, other than a faint echo of the rattling noise.

"Nobody home," Jack said aloud to no one in particular.

He supposed that he could force the door again, go inside, and have a look around. He might even have done it if he'd had a flashlight. But he didn't have a flashlight, and he didn't know where the light switch was.

So he started back to the car.

He'd gone about ten feet when the dog barked.

38

It wasn't a loud bark, just a low, soft woofing sound, but it was definitely made by a dog—a dog that hadn't been in the building the day before and that had no business being in there now.

Oh, sure, there was a minute possibility that the police could have left a guard dog there to look out for things. Jack wondered just how minute the possibility was. He decided that it was about as minute as his chance of picking the winning numbers in Lotto Texas.

It was considerably more likely, about ninety-nine-point-nine percent more, that the dog was the one Estelle had told them about, the mean one that belonged to Ralph Thompson.

And if the dog was there, it was quite possible that Thompson was there, too, lurking in the darkness.

Now why doesn't this make me happy? Jack thought. This was his big chance to impress Sally Good, and he ought to have been elated with the opportunity.

He was standing right beside the sliding door. All he had

to do was pull it aside and go into the store. He'd done it before, and this time, if he got lucky, he might find Ralph Thompson, capture him, and end up a hero.

Or he might be killed by a vicious dog, if Thompson didn't beat him to a pulp first.

Jack decided that he didn't want to take a chance on either of those possibilities. Being a hero was more trouble than it was worth. It was time to use the cell phone.

And that's exactly what he would have done if the door hadn't slid smoothly open, if Ralph Thompson hadn't been standing there, and if the dog hadn't jumped Jack.

Sally tried to claim later that, technically speaking, the dog hadn't jumped him at all, at least not at first. There had been a lot of barking, snapping, gnashing, and maybe even a little nipping, but no jumping.

In the heat of the moment, it didn't matter. The dog, which looked to Jack like a cross between a Siberian husky and a polar bear, was in furious motion all around Jack's legs, his bark echoing off the metal sides of the building, his teeth chomping at Jack's ankles.

So it wasn't surprising that Jack fell down.

When he did, the dog stopped barking and sat on Jack's chest, his pink tongue lapping at Jack's face. Jack put up an arm to fend off the tongue, but it didn't do much good. He was getting a soaking.

Estelle was yelling something that Jack couldn't make out, and Ralph Thompson used the confusion to make a break for it.

Jack rolled to his left, out from under the dog, and stood up. He was almost trampled by Sally, who was running in his direction with both hands extended in front of her.

He couldn't see what she was holding, but he heard her plainly when she yelled, "Freeze, sucker!"

Jack crouched down and put his hands over his ears, expecting to hear the sound of gunshots. The dog, apparently not expecting anything at all, walked over and started licking Jack's face again. The only sound Jack could hear was Estelle, not gunshots.

Jack shoved the dog aside and looked up. Sally stood beside him in a classic shooter's stance, and about fifteen yards away Ralph Thompson stood frozen in place. He looked as if he wanted to take another step but was afraid of what might happen if he did.

Jack stood up. "Did you call 911?"

"Yes," Sally said. "And Estelle has probably aroused the entire neighborhood with her screaming. We should have plenty of help here soon."

The dog licked Jack's hand.

"This is the friendliest dog I've ever seen," Jack said, moving his hand. "I think he barked because he wanted to play, not because he wanted to warn anybody that we were here or because he wanted to attack us."

"I don't know about that," Sally said.

All her attention was concentrated on Thompson. Jack wasn't even sure she'd actually heard what he said.

"Should I go down there and try to do anything?" he asked.

"Don't get close to him. He might try to get the better of you and use you as a hostage. We don't want that."

"No," Jack said. "We don't want that."

"Why don't you put the dog inside? That way, he won't bother the police. Then go see if Coy and Estelle are okay."

Jack did as he was told. After all, Sally was his division chair. Besides, she had a gun.

Putting the dog inside the building was no problem. The dog was only too glad to follow Jack, but it looked sad when he slipped back out and slid the door shut.

When Jack got to the street, Estelle had stopped yelling.

She was talking to Coy, who was still sitting on the back floor of the car.

"I can tell you, they won't be here in less than fifteen minutes," Estelle said. "I called them once about a prowler, and it took them fifteen minutes to get to my house."

"They'll be here," Coy said. "They'll drop everything. Thompson's a killer, after all."

"I hope they get here soon," Jack said. "I don't know how long Sally can hold that gun on Thompson before he makes a break."

"Gun?" Coy said. "What gun?"

"The one Sally got out of the trunk," Jack said.

"I don't know you very well, Jack," Estelle said, "so I hope you won't mind my saying that you must be losing it."

"Yeah," Coy agreed. "We don't know anything about any gun."

"What do you mean?" Jack asked.

"I mean that Sally doesn't have a gun," Coy said. "She didn't take anything out of the trunk."

"Then what's she holding?"

"Oh," Coy said. "That's her cell phone."

Jack felt the bottom of his stomach drop down to his knees. He turned toward Sally, though he didn't really have any clear idea of how to help her. He had taken only one step when he heard sirens.

"Two minutes," Coy said. "Tops."

Estelle snorted. "Well, I guess they think more of you youngsters than they do of a helpless old woman with a prowler running loose in her backyard."

"Did they catch him?" Coy asked.

"No, they did not. He got clean away. By the time they got there, he was probably in Kentucky."

The police car squealed to a stop near Sally's Acura, and one beefy officer got out. Before he had time to ask what the situation was, his backup arrived. Both officers looked questioningly at Jack and Estelle.

"That's Ralph Thompson back there in the dark," Jack said. "Dr. Good's holding him for you."

The officers nodded, drew their sidearms, and began walking toward Sally.

"We're the police," one of them said. "We have everything under control. You can put down the gun, Dr. Good."

Sally bent over and put down the cell phone, and one of the officers stopped to pick it up while the other walked past her toward Thompson.

Jack wished he could have seen the expression of the officer who'd picked up the phone, but the man was facing in the wrong direction.

Sally came back to the car.

"Ever get the drop on anyone with a cell phone before?" Jack asked.

Sally smiled. "You didn't think I'd use my pistol, did you? Someone might get hurt that way."

"What would you have done if Thompson had just kept on running?"

"Ordered a pizza, maybe. Anyway, he didn't run. For all he knew, I really did have a gun. He was more afraid of us than we were of him."

Jack looked into the car where Coy was now sitting in the backseat.

"Some of us were afraid of him," Jack said.

"Not me," Coy said. "I was just being prudent."

Jack might have questioned that, but just about then, Detective Weems drove up.

"It's going to be a long night," Jack said.

Sally just nodded.

39

It wasn't such a long night after all. Weems was eager to get his prisoner to the station, so he didn't bother to question anyone else too closely. And he obviously wanted to get rid of Estelle, who kept asking him why the response time had been so poor when she had called about her prowler.

Sally dropped Jack and Coy off at Jack's car and then drove home, where Lola hissed at her until Sally fed her a kitty treat. After scarfing down the snack, Lola consented to let Sally rub her head, but not for long. After a few seconds, she went off and hid as usual.

Sally didn't mind. She took a long hot shower and thought about all that had happened. After she had gone to bed, she lay awake, going over the events of the last few days in her head.

It seemed obvious now that Ralph Thompson was guilty. In a way, she was glad, because that meant that Jorge was innocent. She really hadn't wanted to think of him as a killer.

Of course, if the rumors were true, he *was* a killer, but that was different. Or so Sally told herself. And even if it wasn't different, Jorge was completely rehabilitated. That was clear to her.

She knew that she should have been happy with the way things had worked out. Jorge, and for that matter the entire college staff, was innocent of Val's death, and Sally had even helped catch the fugitive that the police had been looking for.

She'd also made a new friend in Jack Neville, and she wondered just what the friendship might lead to. Jack was a little strange, but he was also very nice, and he was good to have around in a tight spot. Maybe he wasn't as macho as Jorge, but he wasn't as fainthearted as Coy, either.

She turned over in the bed, and Lola hissed beneath her. Sally hissed back, and went to sleep.

During the next few days, things fell back into their customary routine. Sally graded papers, taught her classes, and did all the things that division chairs had to do: she worked with schedules, advised students, filled out surveys, attended committee meetings, answered phone calls, fiddled with the budget, and signed purchase orders.

The worst problems Sally had to deal with were the usual complaints from students about teachers who, the students were convinced, were grading too harshly, singling them out for criticism, or penalizing them unfairly just because they'd missed class once. Well, okay, maybe twice. Well, okay, for the last three weeks, but they were willing to make up the work they'd missed. Well, most of it. Well, some of it, but only if there was still a chance of making an A in the course.

Sally always listened patiently and tried to explain things clearly and compassionately. However, there were times she wanted to say something like, "Who's paying for you to come to college? Don't you realize you're throwing away their money?"

Sally also had a little talk with Fieldstone about the removal of the painting. He didn't want to talk about it, though he admitted that it had been the wrong thing to do.

"But after it was done," he said, "it was too late to change plans. Besides, if I made a mistake, it was in a good cause. I didn't want Roy Don Talon trying to close us down for being Satanists. And I didn't want him to think he could censor our art."

So you censored it yourself, Sally thought, but she didn't say it. What she did say was, "You should have told me about the painting. I was sure the painting had something to do with Val."

Fieldstone didn't tell Sally that she should have minded her own business, but it was clear that he thought she was the one at fault. She knew that he could never be convinced otherwise, so she didn't pursue it.

The committee that Fieldstone selected looked at the painting, declared it harmless, and reported to Fieldstone, who gave a copy of the report to Roy Don Talon.

Talon came to the campus, had another look at the painting, and left shaking his head, or so Sally heard from Dean Naylor. She expressed her dismay at Naylor's dishonesty, but he claimed the whole thing was Fieldstone's idea.

"Besides," he said, "Val went along with the whole thing."

Sally didn't want to believe that part, but Naylor was convincing. It explained why there had been no ruckus when Jorge had taken the painting, and why Jorge had even signed the guest book when he went into the gallery.

She spoke to Jorge, who told her essentially the same story. She was disappointed in everyone, from Fieldstone to Jorge, but most of all, she was disappointed in Val. Apparently, he'd had no principles at all, even when it came to art.

Jack Neville came by to talk to her at least once a day,

usually to let her know how his article on Bobby Vee was coming along or to complain that Coy Webster still hadn't found his own apartment.

Sally was sure that Jack was going to ask her out soon. She just wished she knew what she was going to say when he did. She put off making that decision until the time came.

All in all, everything on the HCC campus was so normal that it was easy to forget that there had been a murder in the Art Department only a few days earlier.

And then one day, Troy Beauchamp dropped by.

"Did you hear about the confession?" he asked.

Sally said, "Close the door, Troy, and have a seat. And then tell me all about it."

Troy was only too glad to tell. He didn't say how he'd heard, but then he never did. Like any good reporter, he never revealed his sources. Sally suspected, however, that he'd been talking to someone like Chief Desmond, or maybe Tom Clancey.

Troy settled into the uncomfortable chair by Sally's desk and said, "Ralph Thompson has admitted killing his wife."

Sally wasn't surprised. She didn't know what evidence Weems had, but she assumed it was substantial. Otherwise, Thompson would have gotten out of jail on bond.

She asked Troy about it. He knew, of course.

"He killed her with a hammer. The police have it, and there's no doubt it's the murder weapon. Thompson had been hanging piñatas in the back of the store when she came in and told him that she'd reported Val for sexual harassment."

"He didn't like that," Sally said, glad that she and Jack hadn't found the hammer themselves.

"No, he didn't like it. It's pretty complicated, but it seems that Thompson knew his wife was fooling around with Val and had worked out a little blackmail scheme."

Sally said she'd known about the blackmail.

Troy was hurt. "You didn't tell me."

"It wasn't something I thought should get out."

"Well, I suppose I won't hold it against you. What about the fooling around?"

"I didn't know about that."

"I didn't either. I'm amazed, frankly, but it seems that Val had quite a reputation. How could he have been doing those things without my knowing?"

Sally admitted that it was unlikely.

"All those women kept his secrets for him," Troy said. "But I finally found out." He paused. "Anyway, Thompson's wife didn't know about the blackmail scheme. She got scared that she was going to get in trouble for messing around with an instructor, so she decided to say that Val had acted improperly with her."

"He had," Sally said.

"Yes, but Tammi didn't tell the real story. She said he'd touched her when he was working on that painting."

"The painting that was supposed to be for her husband."

"It wasn't for her husband, you know."

"Yes, I did know."

Troy looked disappointed. "Well, it wasn't. According to Thompson, that was just the cover story. It was for Val."

"And that's why Thompson is supposed to have killed Val," Sally said. "He went into a rage when he found out Tammi had ruined his extortion scheme. I heard that he had a terrible temper, and she'd spoiled everything. He was probably sure that he'd be arrested for what he'd done. I can believe that. It pretty much matches up with what some people thought all along."

As she thought about things, however, she still couldn't believe the theory that Thompson had killed Val because of some question of honor. That part still seemed ridiculous to her. She said as much to Beauchamp.

"Ah," Troy said. "You're getting ahead of things. I haven't told you the good part of the story."

"So tell me."

"It's like this," Troy said. "Thompson admits that he killed his wife, and he says he's very sorry about it. He's 'expressing remorse for his crime,' as the newscasters like to say. But he says he didn't kill Val Hurley, and he's not going to say that he did."

"What do the police think?" Sally asked. "Or do you know?"

"Now, what do you think?"

"I think you know. So tell me."

"The police think he's telling the truth. Remember how Val was killed?"

Sally remembered. "He was hit with *Winged Victory*."

Troy smiled. "Right, and there are fingerprints on the statue. But they aren't Ralph Thompson's."

"Whose are they?"

"Ah," Troy said. "That's what the police would like to know."

40

As Troy explained it, all the instructors at the college had been ruled out as suspects because the college had everyone's fingerprints on file.

Sally knew why. Everyone who taught at the prison had to be fingerprinted, and everyone who taught at HCC was required to teach at the prison, or at least to be willing to teach there. So everyone's fingerprints were taken once every two years, and at the same interval, everyone had to endure an "in-service" program about prison security procedures, given by someone from the Texas Department of Criminal Justice.

Sally said, "So that means . . ."

"That means," Troy said, "that you and I aren't guilty."

And neither are A. B. D. Johnson, Coy, Jorge, Ellen, or Vera, Sally thought. *So who is left?*

"I don't know," Troy said when she asked. "And I'll bet they never find out."

"Why?"

"Because who's going to admit it? I don't know of any

clues, so unless someone confesses, whoever killed Val will get off scot-free."

Troy talked for a while longer, but he didn't have any more scoops. When he left, Sally was left to wonder about Val's killer.

It didn't take her long to come up with the answer.

Tammi Thompson.

Sally was sure that was it. She couldn't think of a motive, but that didn't matter. She knew she was right. She picked up her phone and called Chief Desmond.

"You're wrong," Desmond said when she explained the reason for her call. "Do you think the police in Hughes are idiots? The medical examiner took Tammi Thompson's prints at the morgue, and they don't match the ones on the statue."

"Oh," Sally said.

She hung up the phone, and it rang immediately. She picked it up and said, "Sally Good."

Eva Dillon said, "Please hold for Dr. Fieldstone."

Sally didn't say a word. She just waited for Fieldstone, who, naturally, asked her to come over to his office. But this time, he told her why.

"It's about that purchase order to Thompson's Crafts," he said.

"What about it?" Sally asked.

"That's what I want to discuss with you," Fieldstone said.

Sally said that she'd be right over. She knew what was going to happen. Now that the furor about Val's death had died down, someone was going to have to take the fall for the purchase order, and Sally knew who that would be.

It wouldn't be her, but that didn't make her feel any better. Amy Willis was the one who would be fired, though Naylor had as much as said she wouldn't be. That, however, had been when Sally had the upper hand and was protecting Amy. Now, Fieldstone was going to try again.

On her way to see Fieldstone, Sally stopped by Amy Willis's office. Amy was cleaning out her desk, tossing things into a box that had recently held paper for the photocopier. She didn't seem to care whether the things fit in the box neatly. She didn't even seem to care whether the things went in it at all. A framed photo of her son hit the edge of the box and bounced onto the desk. Amy didn't bother to pick it up.

Sally did. She said, "I'm sorry, Amy."

Amy looked around. She was nervous and distracted. Her hands went to her hair, as if she were reaching for the pencil that was usually stuck there. Today, it was gone.

"I knew it was coming," she said. "I knew they wouldn't let me off so easily. But it wasn't my fault. It was Val's fault."

"I know that," Sally said.

And then a number of things clicked into place in Sally's head. She knew how meticulous Amy was, and she remembered what Amy had said in Fieldstone's office, about how she'd known there was a mistake, but she had waited too long to figure it out. Sally wondered now if that was true. And while Amy was naturally the nervous sort, since Val's death she'd been about three times as nervous as usual.

There was something else, too, something that Amy had said—or hadn't said—in Fieldstone's office. Thinking back on it, Sally believed that Amy had been about to say, "That's what I *wanted* to know," but she'd changed the verb to the present tense. That was something an English teacher should have thought of sooner.

Sally said, "Amy, did you go to Val's office and ask Val about the purchase order?"

Amy stiffened. "Me? Why are you asking me that?"

"Because it seems like the kind of thing you'd do. You

243

wouldn't call me first. Dr. Fieldstone mentioned the other day about how conscientious you are. You'd check that purchase order out. You'd ask Val. You did ask him, didn't you? And the next day, you called me to cover for yourself."

Amy sat down. She wasn't nervous now. She was hardly moving.

"No," she said. "I didn't do those things. I should have talked to Val, but I didn't."

"I think you did," Sally said. "If you did, someone saw you going over to the Art and Music Building. Douglas Young, maybe. He sees everything. Or maybe Coy Webster. He might have met you as he was leaving that day."

Amy's eyes dropped at the mention of Coy's name. Sally knew that Coy must have seen her, but not while he was in the building. He'd been leaving it and hadn't thought anything about someone from the Business Office being on the way in. He might not even have remembered it.

"The police have your fingerprints, too," Sally said. "They were on the statue you hit Val with."

While the faculty members had to be fingerprinted, the members of the staff did not. They weren't required to go to the prison. So if Amy hadn't committed any other crimes, her fingerprints weren't on file anywhere at all.

Amy started to sniffle. "It was just that Val didn't seem to care. I told him I was probably going to lose my job, and he just shrugged. He told me that he had problems of his own and that my troubles didn't amount to a thing compared to his. I lost my temper then. That little statue was right there, and I grabbed it and hit him with it. I was angry, and I meant to hurt him, but not to kill him. I never meant to do that."

"I believe you," Sally said, reaching for the telephone.

Later that day, after a long session of Minesweeper, Jack Neville went by Sally's office.

"The news is all over campus," he said. "About how you caught the killer, that is. You don't look too happy about it, though."

"I'm not," Sally said. "Amy didn't intend to kill anyone. Now she's going to prison, and it's my fault. What's going to happen to her son?"

"First of all," Jack said, "it's not your fault. You didn't kill anyone. There's plenty of blame in this thing, but none of it's yours. Blame Val if you want to. He's the one who let himself be blackmailed. Blame Ralph Thompson for blackmailing him. Blame Tammi for getting involved with Val. Blame Vera or Ellen for not telling you about Val sooner. But don't blame yourself."

Sally tried to smile. "You're right," she said.

"Of course I am. And as far as Amy's son goes, her ex-husband has been trying to get custody for quite a while. He's always been a good father."

"But what about Amy?"

"She might not go to prison. There are lots of possibilities. She could plead temporary insanity, for one thing. She was pushed over the edge by the faked purchase order and her fear of losing her job and her son. It's the kind of thing that might sway a jury."

"Maybe," Sally said, though she didn't really believe it.

"You need something to take your mind off all this," Jack said. "There's an, ah, oldies concert this weekend, headlined by the Platters. There might even be one or two of the original members left."

"So?" Sally said.

"So, ah, would you like to go with me?"

Sally thought about it.

Would she like to go with him?

Yes.

Should she?

Probably not. It was against her policy. Besides, dating a member of the department was a lot worse than dating anyone else at the college.

On the other hand, maybe it was time to take a chance.

"I'd love to," she said.